Moonkid and Prometheus

Stoddart Publishing gratefully acknowledges the support
of the Canada Council and the Ontario Arts Council
in the development of writing and publishing in Canada.

Published in Canada in 1997 by Stoddart Kids,
a division of Stoddart Publishing Co. Limited
34 Lesmill Road
Toronto, Canada M3B 2T6
Tel (416) 445-3333 Fax (416) 445-5967
e-mail Customer.Service@ccmailgw.genpub.com

Published in the United States in 1998 by Stoddart Kids
85 River Rock Drive, Suite 202
Buffalo, New York 14207
Toll free 1-800-805-1083
e-mail gdsinc@genpub.com

Cover art: Sharif Tarabay
Cover design Tannice Goddard

Canadian Cataloguing in Publication Data

Kropp, Paul, 1948–
Moonkid and Prometheus

ISBN 0-7736-7465-9

I. Title.

PS8571.R772M66 1997   jC813'.54   C97-930338-9
PZ7.K76M66 1997

Printed and bound in Canada

MOONKID AND PROMETHEUS

PAUL KROPP

Stoddart Kids

Chapter 1

"You're a what?" my sister Liberty asked in that mocking voice of hers. It's the one she uses when she wants to annoy me.

"A tutor," I said.

"A tooter. Like you've taken up the flute?" she replied, playing dumber than she actually is.

"A tutor," I explained. "Noun, singular. As in, a person who gives additional or remedial instruction."

"Ian, I always knew you'd make an excellent human dictionary," she began. Libby was smiling in a seemingly pleasant way while running a brush through her dark, shoulder-length hair. "But as for being a tutor, well, that requires social skills . . . " She paused, with the obvious implication.

"I have social skills," I told her, my voice rising. "When I want to."

"Which is why you have so many friends," she said, applying a lipstick of some ghastly, decayed beebleberry color. "You do have friends, don't you, Ian? Why, I'd need the fingers of both hands to count them all . . . "

I waited. I knew there'd be a punch line.

" . . . if I were a double amputee." She pulled her sleeves down over her hands and grinned at me.

"Libby, why don't you stop hassling your brother?" my father spoke up. He was sitting in full lotus position on the floor, obviously in mid-meditation, somewhere between the 240th and 241st repetition of his mantra. It was highly unusual for him to interrupt the morning journey towards Nirvana just to climb into the middle of an argument between Libby and me. Maybe he realized just how unfair Libby was being. After all, I really had been working on my social skills, or at least trying to get along better with ordinary humans since all that trouble two years ago.

"So sorry," Libby replied breezily. "I was just wondering what he was up to, that's all. Why this sudden urge to do good, Ian? You decide to stop talking about your social conscience and actually do something with it?"

"Libby . . . " my father cautioned.

"Actually, I had some encouragement," I told her.

"Encouragement?" my father asked, staring right at me.

"Maybe a little stronger than encouragement," I admitted. "A kind of strong suggestion. Mrs. Greer, the vice-principal, said she thought I'd be better off doing something besides sitting in the cafeteria on my spare period."

"So why were you talking to the VP?" Libby asked. "You two just decide to do lunch or are you in trouble again?" From the look on her face, Libby already knew the answer.

"Just a little trouble."

The two of them stared at me. My father had this dubious expression on his face that made him look like a long-haired Alfred E. Neuman, without the freckles. Obviously that's where I get my remarkable good looks. My sister had arched one of her carefully-plucked eyebrows, giving her an expression of absolute disbelief and scorn. It's something she probably picked up from *Cosmopolitan* or *Elle*.

"Okay, more than a little trouble." I sighed. "My math and gym teachers are ganging up on me. And there's this kid named Ryan. And I spilled a little soup in the cafeteria the other day."

"You had to see the VP for spilled soup?" my dad asked.

"Well, I kind of accidentally spilled it on this guy Ryan."

They stared at me. Both of Libby's eyebrows were now arched in disbelief.

"Okay, maybe it wasn't a hundred percent accidental. Maybe it was fifty percent unconscious and fifty percent accidental."

"Maybe it was fifty percent you being obnoxious," Libby said, "and fifty percent you being stupid. And I thought you'd shown signs of almost becoming normal, Ian. Like, almost human." Libby gave me this look. "Didn't Greer already warn you about getting in trouble?"

"She did," I said. Actually, when Mrs. Greer pulled out the file, it seemed she had warned me about "getting along with others" on five different occasions, but I wasn't going to admit that to Libby. This business of being human was proving to be a lot more difficult than I'd expected. Maybe I should have stuck to my fantasy of being a somewhat lost but highly competent alien.

"So what's the deal? What's your penance for spilled soup, Ian?"

"I'm supposed to tutor some kid at the elementary school," I said.

"Ian," my father told me, "I think this tutoring could be a very good thing." He gave me the wonderful, half-spaced-out smile that always warmed my heart.

"Yeah," Libby added, "it'll give you a chance to practice your primitive social skills on some kid who's so dumb he won't know any better."

"Thanks, Lib, I really appreciate that," I shot back at her.

"Would you two just cool it," my father said, his voice less mellow than before.

"No problem," Libby replied as she moved her skinny body over to the door. "And what if this tutoring thing doesn't work out?" she asked me. "I assume Greer didn't make the tutoring a fun-sy thing you could pick up or leave aside as you see fit? That's not her style."

"Well, no," I said. My voice caught in my throat.

"So?" Libby asked.

"Well, unless things work out better, I mean, with the tutoring and all . . . I get bounced."

"Bounced?" my father asked.

"Transferred," I explained. "They're going to transfer me to Markdale for what she calls 'a fresh start.'"

"Markdale Secondary!?" my sister said, in the kind of tone that seems to call for both a question mark and an exclamation point. "They'll eat you alive at Markdale. They'll take a short, snotty kid like you, chew you up for lunch and spit you out by fourth period."

"Is Markdale that bad a school?" my dad asked.

"Markdale isn't a bad school, Rick," she began, calling my father by his first name the way we always do, "it's the armpit of the school district. It's worse — it's the sweat gland of the armpit of the district. It's —"

"Look," I broke in, "it doesn't matter. I'm not going to Markdale. I'm going to tutor this kid and get along with the guys at school and make Mrs. Greer happy. There's no reason to go wild with the metaphors, Lib. I'm working it out. As a matter of fact, I see it as an opportunity. A kind of second chance."

There was silence. Libby gave me this look, some mix of disbelief and bewilderment and compassion. My father shook his head, sighed, and stared at me like I was a five-year-old who'd been caught stealing gum at the variety store.

Finally Libby spoke. "Ian," she said, "just don't mess up the tutoring, okay? Greer doesn't give third chances."

"I won't mess up."

"Because if you end up at Markdale . . . " She paused and thought about it. "Well, maybe we can get a deal on a really small casket."

* * *

So I started off that morning with more than the usual level of frustration and irritation, probably an 8.3 on the ten-point F&I scale. Second period, my F&I numbers had gone down to a more reasonable 5.6. I decided to keep them that way by not taking my spare in the cafeteria. Why give Ryan and his gang of resident wits the chance to comment upon my size (which is somewhat small), my ears (which are somewhat large), my freckles (which are rather numerous), my I.Q. (which is astronomical, at least on the verbal score) or my parentage (my father's reputation lives on despite recent respectability)? Instead, I headed down Shuter Street until I came to the crumbling concrete steps that led to Fairfield Middle School.

The doors ahead of me were painted a bright red, festooned with knifed initials and spray-painted gang names. The door windows had been reinforced with a kind of chicken-wire, maybe to keep the kids inside securely cooped up, maybe to keep the three winos staggering on the sidewalk safely outside.

I followed the Visitors Must Report signs to the main office, then stood at the counter while two secretaries continued an animated conversation centered on last night's made-for-TV movie. While I stood there bouncing on the balls of my feet, they kept talking. The plight of Meredith Baxter-Birney at the hands of her made-for-TV abusive husband was obviously a lot more interesting than I was. Occasionally, they punctuated their key ideas with the pop of bubblegum bubbles.

After a while, I coughed my most polite please - look-up-and-notice-me cough, but their gum chewing and animated discussion didn't skip a beat. Finally I coughed again, this time bringing up enough phlegm that the nicely polished floors of Fairfield Middle School might well be in trouble if I did anything with it.

One secretary cast a bored eye or two in my direction. "What were you sent down for?" she asked.

"Sent down?" I said. It took a minute for the realization to hit — she thought I was a student at their school. An *elementary school* student!

The secretary took my astonished silence as a failure to comprehend her question. She repeated the gist of it: "What did ya do?"

"Nothing," I said, suddenly feeling guilty for some sin I'd never committed — throwing rocks in the playground, painting my teacher's name in candy-apple red on the sandbox, flying a kite without a city permit. "I'm from the high school. I'm here to be a tutor." I tried to say the last line with authority, but it still came out as if there were a question mark at the end. A tutor? Me?

"What's your name?" the secretary asked, parking her gum in one cheek. It gave her a kind of deformed chipmunk air.

"Ian McNaughton."

She turned to look at a sheet on the corner of her desk, then stared back at me, perhaps with a newfound sense of my maturity and stature. After all, I was a committed, community-minded high school student, wasn't I? Or maybe she was just amazed that someone as short as I am might actually be enrolled in secondary school.

"Who?" she asked.

"McNaughton, comma, Ian," I said, and then began spelling it out. "M . . . C . . . N . . . "

"Oh, here you are," she said, some ten-watt bulb turning on inside her brain as she found my name on a list. "You're supposed to go see Ms. Noble in Room 103. I'll call her on the P.A. and say you're coming."

I walked along the hall from the office, past 108 where the teacher was screaming at the top of her lungs, past 106 where one little kid was putting modeling clay into the hair of another little kid, past 104 where the teacher was showing an Indiana Jones movie, to 103, the classroom where I was to work.

I knocked. The door opened and an enormous woman stood in front of me. She was so large she virtually filled the door frame, blocking the brightness of the windows behind her like a human eclipse of the sun.

"You're the one from the high school?" she asked.

"Uh, yeah," I said. I admit that my jaw was hanging open. It was just that I had never in my life encountered a teacher of such incredible size. She was an ocean liner compared to the little tug-boats of teachers I'd had in the past. "I mean, yes, ma'am. I'm here to tutor one of your students."

"That's right," she said, as if my answer deserved full marks. From the classroom behind her, there was a small noise — a kid giggling, or popping gum, or committing some other affront to elementary school order. Ms. Noble turned and stared into her room with such power that an ominous silence was restored. You could have heard the proverbial clock tick, if clocks still ticked, and were it not for the Indiana Jones video in the next classroom.

When the enforced silence had gone on long enough to make all of us uncomfortable, Ms. Noble motioned to a student. "Pro, could you come here, please?"

From one of the desks an enormous kid stood up. The boy was only in grade seven, but he was already six feet tall even without the high-top haircut that added an extra inch or two.

"Pro, this is . . . " There was a pause while Ms. Noble searched her memory for my name, which must have been sent to her by the guidance office. Finally she gave up. "This is your tutor from the high school."

"Ian," I said, smiling in what I hoped was an engaging way.

The kid said nothing and seemed to be looking at the floor, which was highly polished but otherwise not terribly interesting. But I sympathized. Looking at Ms. Noble was a fairly daunting task and looking at me was something most humans avoided.

"Maybe you two could go down to the library and get acquainted," Ms. Noble suggested, much as an army sergeant suggests that a new recruit spit-shine his boots one more time. "Pro, you know the way."

The kid nodded and moved past me out to the hall. I followed after him, feeling a bit like a small dog at the end of a parade. We walked past four classrooms, then turned left and went down a corridor that smelled strongly of wet running shoes, and opened the door to a room marked Library that seemed to have only a handful of books and no librarian or other adult in sight.

The kid moved to an old couch in the center of the room and sprawled on it. I sat down on a hard wooden chair that was at right angles to the couch. Neither of us talked. There was an awkward silence for some chunk of eternity, and then the kid really looked at me for the first time.

"So what you s'posed to do for me, man?" He just sat there, an oversized lump of pre-teen arrogance, as if he were quite all right and I must have some kind of problem.

Why was I surprised? Did I actually think the kid would greet me with mannered civility — "Yes, good sir, it's so splendid of you to give up your time to assist me in my school work?" Fat chance!

"I'm supposed to be helping you with your reading," I said at last.

"I can read," the kid announced. "I can read half the stuff in this library. If I felt like it."

That was an opening for me. "I'll help you read

the other half," I said.

"Maybe I don't want to," the kid replied. His words came out quickly: *mebbe-I-doan-wanna*. Then he added the kicker. "Maybe it don't matter to me."

That threw me. How could anybody say that reading didn't matter? Ignoring the fact that books constitute the basis of civilization, culture, technology and everything else on this planet, consider the alternative — a life defined by reruns of *Gilligan's Island*, regular showings of *Wheel of Fortune* and the occasional video epic along the lines of *Buffy, the Vampire Slayer*. Maybe I should have said something like that. Instead, I countered with a line that belonged in some kind of TV sitcom.

"Listen, don't you want to get good marks in school?" Pathetic, I thought, as soon as I'd said it. Might as well stick an ice cream cone on my forehead.

"I get good marks. But not in reading. Reading is boring, man. You open this book, and the teacher say read page thirty-two out loud and so you get to page thirty-two and there's this stupid poem, about daff'dils or something. Why should I read a bunch of stuff about daff'dils? I can't tell a daff'dil from a dandelion, you know? Like who cares? Or you open some book, some story book, and it ain't even real. I mean, how come I should read something that ain't real?"

"Well, sometimes a story or a novel can be realer than real life," I said.

"That don't make sense," the kid announced, and I realized that it didn't, even though it was probably true.

"Listen, I'm not here to argue with you," I said, backing off. "We're supposed to be getting acquainted and I don't even know your name yet."

"Pro," he said.

"Pro? Is that it? Like pro basketball or pro baseball?"

"Yeah, kind of," he said. "Listen, Mr. Tutor, what they call you?"

"Ian," I said. "Ian McNaughton."

"They call you Ian?"

I thought for a second. Certainly my family called me Ian, except for my sister who used to refer to me as Garlic-breath or Elephant-ears but lately has moved on to more sophisticated nick-names. But at school nobody except the teachers used my real name, and I figured it wouldn't hurt to tell Pro the nickname they preferred.

"They call me Moonkid."

He smiled. "How come?"

"Because my middle name is Callisto. It's one of the moons of Jupiter. And because I look a little weird, like I belong on some other planet. When I was a kid, I even thought I was *from* another planet. You know, sent here for some mission they'd forgotten to tell me about."

He laughed. "That's cool, man. Maybe they sent you down here to tutor somebody like me."

That seemed doubtful. Surely any self-respecting alien planet would have devised a bigger mission for yours truly than trying to help this lummox of kid. But it wasn't as if I had any choice in the matter.

"So what's your real name?" I asked.

"Prometheus," he replied. "Prometheus John Gibbs. Prometheus, he's a Greek god. And John's after my old man, and Gibbs's the family name. Except nobody around here can say Prometheus so they call me Pro. It's cool."

"Yeah, it is," I said. Cooler than Moonkid. Light-years cooler.

"So you got a family?" Prometheus asked me.

I realized at this point that the interview had turned around — the tutee was finding out more about the tutor than vice-versa, but at least we were talking.

"A sister," I said. "She goes to university. And my father runs a bookstore in the west end called Rick's Bookroom." I left out my mother. She hardly counted, anyhow.

"No wonder you want me to read, man," Prometheus said. Now the grin on his face was wider and showed the pointed teeth at the back of his mouth. "Your old man could sell some books to me."

"Yeah, I guess," I agreed. The simplicity of the

explanation had a certain appeal, though Prometheus looked an unlikely customer for the kind of books my father stocked. It was hard to picture him browsing through the *Collected Letters of Nathanial Hawthorne*, for instance, or getting caught up in proposals for a Marxist paradise on earth. "So how about you read something for me, then we can say we did something when Ms. Noble comes back?"

"S'pose I don't wanna?"

"Suit yourself. But you said you could read half the books here," I reminded him, finally using my brains instead of TV clichés.

"You don't believe what I say?" he snapped at me, the smile disappearing.

"Sure I do," I told him. "But I'd believe it more if I could see it."

Prometheus had stopped looking at me. His eyes were off to the left, aimed at the floor or the bottom of a magazine rack. His foot was moving nervously. I figured I could fit my whole head inside one of his size-thirteen Converse running shoes.

"So what you reading, man? Betcha I could read that," he said.

I shook my head. "I'm doing something called *A Tale of Two Cities* for school," I said.

"Lemme have it," he ordered.

I suppose I could have said something right away about it being a school book, about grade ten

English being a galaxy away from grade seven reading, about the density of Charles Dickens' writing. But I didn't. Explanation would have been awkward and we were still trying to get past that. So I reached in my pack and handed him my copy.

Prometheus stared at the cover, a stylized drawing of a seventeenth-century French soldier, then flipped to page one. I watched his eyes as they focused on the print. His lips moved silently, then he began, "'It was the best of times, it was the worst of times, it was the age of wis-dom, it was the age of fool . . . fool-ishness.'" Prometheus looked up at me, obviously proud of himself. "'It was the ep . . . ep . . . e-poach —'"

"Epoch," I corrected.

"Right, 'epoch of belief, it was the epoch of . . . '" Pro's voice dropped off, but he kept the book high in front of his face, pretending to read the rest of the page. After thirty seconds or so of faking it, he tossed the book down.

"It's boring, man," he announced.

"Takes a while to get into it," I said. "So why not pick something you want to read?"

"Nothin' I wanna read," he said, folding his arms over his chest.

"So how about this?" I said, quickly searching a shelf nearby for something with big print and small words. I came up with a book called *Tough Stuff*.

"That's too easy," Prometheus announced,

opening the book to the middle and cracking the spine.

"Show me how easy," I said, cajoling.

Prometheus looked at me, then back to the book, then away. He thought for a second, took a deep breath, and focused back on the book. He began, "'Tiff swung back towards the ladder.'" He looked up at me. "That's a funny name, Tiff, you know?"

"Yeah. So maybe you could read a little more?" I prompted.

"Sure, man, this is real easy," he said, and then began reading. "'She got it with her feet. She seemed . . . frozen up there, her feet stuck in the ladder, her hands were . . . de-de . . . '"

He was stuck on a word, but the way he was holding the book I couldn't see the text. I offered a guess. "Desperately?"

"Yeah, 'desperately holding onto the rope. Jake was . . . yelling something to her, but Tiff . . . could . . . couldn't move.' There, that's enough." He closed the book.

"So I guess you can read."

"Yeah, I can read. But not that good, you know? That's what Ms. Noble, she tells me. She say —"

Prometheus didn't get a chance to finish. He looked up and out at the doorway with an intensity that made me look out as well.

There was a kid standing there, a skinny kid in shorts and a T-shirt with a Blue Jays cap on his head. One of his legs had a large, discolored scar as if he'd been in some awful accident as a baby.

"Hey, Pro, you can't read, man," the kid drawled. "You're stupid as cow spit, and every-body knows it."

Prometheus was quick coming back. "Shut your face up, Z-Boy. You keep runnin' off at the mouth and maybe I gotta start beatin' your head, man."

The skinny kid just laughed at the threat. "Jus' like you beat that guy who mouthed off 'bout Tina, eh? Think you're tough as your old man, but you ain't."

Pro was up on his feet, a terrible look on his face. "You shut up, Z-Boy —"

"Why don't you tell whitey 'bout Tina, man? Tell him about old Mount Olympus. Tell him what it's really —"

The kid wasn't able to finish, which was probably just as well because Prometheus looked like he was about to slug him in the face. As it was, both the kid and Prometheus were cut short by the sudden appearance of the enormous Ms. Noble. She came up behind Z-Boy and put her hand down on his skinny shoulder.

"Aren't you supposed to be in class, Zed?" Ms. Noble asked.

"Yes'm," he replied.

"Maybe you better get there before I talk to Mr. Donaldson."

"Yes'm."

"*Now*, Zed," she said ominously.

"Yes'm." And the kid disappeared as quickly as he had shown up.

Ms. Noble eased into the library like an ocean liner sailing into port. I was more than a little awed.

"Have you two had a chance to get acquainted?" she asked.

Prometheus and I spoke at the same time. "Yes'm." She must have heard the identical contraction several hundred times a day.

"I brought along an extra copy of Pro's reader," Ms. Noble said, putting lots of emphasis on the *read*. "I thought this might be a good place to start."

"We already started, ma'am," Prometheus told her. "I read one of his books."

"Well, that's good, Pro. But I think it might be best if . . . " She looked at me, trying to remember my name. " . . . your tutor helped you with what we're doing in class. I've marked the selection."

Ms. Noble handed me a copy of a green textbook called *Springboards for Reading Achievement* that I remembered from one of my old elementary schools. As I recalled, the book was considerably less bouncy than its title would suggest.

"And since you still have a few minutes," Ms. Noble went on, "perhaps this young man could help you complete your journal entry for today. All you've written so far is the date." She handed

Pro an official Education District ruled notebook.

"But nothin' happened to me since yesterday," Pro complained. "I don't got nothin' to write about."

"Oh, yes you do," replied Ms. Noble. "You've got a tutor from the high school now. Perhaps you could write about him."

Prometheus frowned for a second, maybe wondering if further complaining would get him out of the assignment. But then he looked down at my somewhat oversized cheeks, or my ears, or something that made him smile, and he picked up a pencil.

Chapter 2

Journal. Sep 16

Today, a kid from high school come to ~~tutr~~ tutor
me how to read better. His name is Ian but ~~everb~~
they call him Moonkid. He look like a Moonkid
too. He got big ears that kind of flap out from his
head. He got these big cheeks, like he got an apple
stuck in them. He got ~~freklo~~ freckles, too, that
make him look dum. He says that everybody on
his ~~plannott~~ planet look like him. He says that he
be a real dude someplace in the ~~uni~~ universe, but
not here. Everybody just laff at him here.

So I show him I can read good ~~al~~ already, but he
still going to help me. He act real smart and
maybe he thinks I'm real stupid. But he's wrong.
I'm going to show him.

Chapter 3

"So how'd it go?" Libby asked me the next morning. She had managed to apply peach-colored lipstick to both lips and one tooth, but I resisted the temptation to say anything.

"Fine," I said.

"Fine?"

"Fine."

There was a silence after this relatively stupid exchange. I decided to break it. "All right, maybe it was a little weird, but I'll get used to it. This kid's got a bit of an attitude problem."

"Makes you a good match. What's his name?"

"Prometheus."

Another silence.

"His name is Prometheus," I repeated.

She stopped and gave me a look, probably

wondering if I was being as sarcastic to her as she was to me. "Really?" she said.

"Really," I told her. "I'm supposed to help him with reading and language arts."

"That makes sense. The poor kid will need advanced literacy skills just to write his own name." Libby grabbed her leather jacket from the chair. "What are you doing with him?"

"Yesterday I helped with the spelling in his journal."

"What did he write about? Abuse in the home? Drugs in the urban jungle? How I learned to do crack over my summer vacation?"

"Actually, he wrote about me."

My sister shot me a smile as she walked to the door. "Kind of a *short* subject, eh?" And then she was out the door before I could get even with her.

I should explain that Libby's humor has gotten nastier as her politics have moved to the right, two tendencies I've noticed since she started at university. Any day I expect her to announce that she has joined the campus investment club and decided to become a business major. Actually, these would be wise moves for someone whose main goals in life are to wear expensive clothing and marry a man who drives a Porsche 924.

I should point out that Libby hasn't always been like this. Even two years ago, during my father's great porno scandal, Libby was solidly on side with us. She even managed to resist the lure of my mother, the Queen of Conspicuous Consumption, who was ready to take her out to the posh life of California. Libby said no back then. These days, I'm not so sure what she'd do. She seems to have one foot planted in the lefty-Liberal values she was born into, and one foot about to land somewhere to the right of Rush Limbaugh — an awkward posture, to say the least.

My own feet, hammer toes and all, are firmly planted on the left, that Pinko-bleeding-heart-Liberal position that upholds the importance of justice and compassion — despite a larger society that mostly rewards greed and ruthlessness. Sadly, greed and ruthlessness seem to be winning, at least in politics.

When I got to school, I ended up walking by Mrs. Greer, who had taken up her famous *I stand on guard for thee* stance in the front hall. She looked like one of those overweight sopranos in a Wagner opera, minus the ram's horns, of course.

"Ian," she said, stopping me abruptly, "how was your first day at Fairfield?"

"Okay," I said, but then realized she wanted something a little more positive. Mrs. Greer is the kind of woman who expects happiness to be marked with a broad smile, and success to be accompanied by brass bands. "I mean, it was great," I said, grinning from large ear to large ear.

"Glad it went well. You stick with it, now.

Remember our deal."

"Yes'm," I said, wiping the sweat off my brow. As if I could forget.

Now I will not pretend that I am one-hundred-percent thrilled with my current high school, Donlands S.S. A mostly-drab faculty delivers a mostly-dull curriculum to a mostly-bored group of students. And I will admit that I have a certain problem getting along with my fellow students, a problem which has dogged me since elementary school, if not before. ("From birth, Ian," my sister says. "You've been a social loser since the cradle.") The problem with high school is that one's social outcast status seems so much more . . . well, obvious.

This year, for instance, it was my fate to be assigned a locker between those of Jessica Smith-Weir and Genevieve Boucher. Were I one of the popular group here, stashing my stuff between two of the most beautiful women in the school would be a source of great pleasure. As things stand, my locker constitutes a daily reminder of how insignificant I am in the social flow at Donlands S.S.

"Gen, did you hear about what happened at Jake's party?" Jessica speaks as she applies lipstick to lips like slices of pear.

"No, I was at Adam's. Like what? What happened?" Genevieve is combing dark hair that ought to belong to a Polynesian princess.

I am between them. Invisible. Because of my height, I am at the level of Jessica's navel which is staring at me from the revealed midriff between her blouse and her jeans. If lust has a temperature, I am near boiling.

"Megan got bombed again and started coming on to — you'll never guess." Jessica puckers her lips in the mirror. My temperature rises a degree.

"Who? Not Ryan. She's not that desperate." Genevieve is interested now, looking at Jessica over the top of my head as I pretend to search for a notebook.

"No." Jessica pauses for effect. "Steve Smiley."

"*Ohmygod*!" says Genevieve. "She must have been, like, so bombed. I mean, Steve Smiley, like he doesn't even *exist*."

They laugh. I close my locker, looking at both of them, wondering if there is anything I could say to get their attention, anything that wouldn't be absolutely pathetic. They are already laughing at Steve Smiley, who plays three sports and whose father is a partner in a distinguished law firm. If Steve Smiley doesn't *exist*, then I am a Cretaceous slug crawling along the volcanic shore trying to breathe. I am an amoeba trying to make my way up the evolutionary scale to paramecium. I am less — I am a food vacuole.

My day does not improve. In a semestered school, we have only four periods a day. Mine begins with biology, goes to math, then phys. ed.

after lunch and a spare last period where I've scheduled the tutoring. I don't get my good subjects — English, history, geography, art — until next semester. So I suffer through examinations of dissected mice in biology, attempt to compute the areas of rhomboids and parallelograms in math, and finish my day with some bone-crushing sport in the gym. Today, the sport is baseball.

Twenty of us troop out to the back field where some civic-minded citizen has donated a baseball diamond in the memory of his dog, or his mother, or someone with the unfortunate name of Flossie. We stand around idly while our overweight gym teacher, Mr. Newman — known affectionately as Fred, though sometimes called *Das Fuhrer* because of his German accent — speaks knowledgeably about batting technique. I try to pay attention, knowing there will be a multiple-choice quiz on Friday (if only the teacher would set essay questions!), and fully aware that my *performance* and *participation* marks (referred to as 'pp' by the students, as in, "How's your pee pee?") are less than stratospheric.

Then we have one of those distressing sports rituals — choosing up. The teacher appoints two captains, invariably jocks whose rippling muscles and deft coordination would make them first picks anyway, and then the rest of the class lines up. Those with talent in the particular sport are selected first: "Ryan," calls one captain. Ryan smiles triumphantly, his status confirmed by being first-pick. The other captain looks frustrated, scans the line, then calls, "Bill." The first captain and Ryan exchange notes, calling for Josh, who can't run but can certainly hit. The second captain calls for Skye, an enormous student with a gold tooth, rumored to have been arrested for armed robbery, and certainly the strongest guy in class.

Now that the talent has been spoken for, the students remaining have to jostle for attention. "Hey, man, pick me," says Bronson. "Ryan, c'mon," begs Jay. They are picked, on a pecking order of who-knows-who, and who can maybe run to catch a ball without falling flat on his face. I make neither list. Additionally, I have that soup-related problem with Ryan who refuses to even look in my direction.

At the end — and this is the worst part — only two or three guys remain. The lame and the halt. There is Trevor, who hates sports; Willie, who weighs three-hundred pounds; and me. The three phys. ed. misfits.

"I'll take Willie if we get a pinch runner," says one captain.

A nod. The second captain stares back and forth between Trevor and me. Trevor is posturing, trying to look confident. I am trying to climb into my running shoes.

There is a general look of dismay among the others on the team. What a choice! Finally the captain and Ryan make up their minds. "Okay, Moonkid, I guess it's you." There's laughter and I go walking over, my only solace that I was second-last-pick and not last, as is so often the case.

We play baseball. The teacher pitches to both teams, my only piece of good fortune, because Fred throws the softball slow enough that I can at least see the thing. In two turns at bat, I manage to tick the ball twice — both fouls — before striking out. This was as expected. The top of the order are expected to hit big and score the runs, and they do. Someone out there is keeping score: 15-15. We are at bat. The class is almost at an end. Jay has been stranded on third by an out at first base. Our team is at the bottom of the batting order. Me.

"Pinch hitter," pleads Ryan.

There are shouts and objections from the other team. *Das Fuhrer* rules: "No pinch hitters. Next batter in the order."

The team looks at me with despair as I step out towards the plate. There are three bats of different sizes and weights on the ground. In despair myself, I pick up the largest and heaviest bat. In the face of doom, I will fight well-armed.

"Bunt it," hisses one guy.

"Just swing easy," says another.

Fred pitches the ball to me, slowly, so that it bounces on the base. Ball. Fred throws again, faster, looking good — and I swing. Too soon.

"C'mon, Moonkid," shouts somebody on our

team. I can feel all of them watching me: eighteen eyeballs drilling into me, all looking for a miracle.

Fred pitches the ball again, a good one. Wait for it, wait for it. Oh, no.

"Strike two," Fred calls. I didn't even swing.

Fifteen-fifteen. Man on third in striking distance. Two men out. Two strikes on the batter. The situation, as they say, is tense. A chant goes up from the other team: "MOONKID! MOONKID! MOONKID!" I could bunt the ball. I could crowd the base and try to get a hit. I could fall down and fake an epileptic fit.

"It's hopeless," says Ryan. He's covered his face with his hands.

"Just *hit* it," screams our captain, red in the face.

"You're meat," whispers the catcher.

I pat the base with the tip of the bat, get in position, and squint out to see Fred winding up. The pitch is coming — another good one — and maybe, just maybe —

"He *hit* it!" screams our captain.

"Ohmygod! Ohmygod!" shouts Ryan.

I am stunned. I have actually hit the ball. It is sailing over Fred's head, over the second baseman. Someone is shouting, "Run, run!" but I can't believe what's happened. I hit the ball. I HIT THE BALL!

From third, Jay is running home but I'm still transfixed by the ball, by its arc in the sky, by the way someone out there is moving towards it. Who is that? Trevor? He's so uncoordinated he can barely button his shirt. He couldn't —

He does. There's a roar from the other team, an astonished smile on Trevor's face as the ball lands smack in his glove, and my first hit in an eternity of hitless games turns into an easy out.

* * *

"So what's wrong with you, man?" Prometheus said right off the bat, to use a now-obnoxious pun. We were sitting in a small conference room off the office, ejected from the library because the teacher in 105 had joined the teacher in 106 for a video extravaganza.

"Nothing," I said.

"C'mon, guy," Pro pressed, "nobody looks like that for nothin'."

"Looks like what?"

"Like you just stepped in a pile of it, you know? Like your great aunt Millie just died and didn't leave you nothin'. You know what I mean." Prometheus was smiling, perhaps in an attempt to cheer me up.

"Listen, this is a tutoring session, right? Not a therapy hour," I snapped at him. "So I had a bad day, all right? It happens. Now where's that book you're supposed to read? *Springboards* to something-or-other."

"Beats me, man."

I finally found the green textbook Ms. Noble had given me, then saw a hint of the same green in Prometheus' book bag. I pulled it out. "So what are you supposed to be reading? Which selection?" I flinched when I said that, sounding so much like a teacher. Only in school do people read selections.

"'The Monkey's Paw,'" Prometheus said, his smile fading. "It's s'posed to be scary, but it ain't."

I opened to the page. "You read it yet? I mean, since you can read so well." I guess there was more than a little sarcasm in the last bit.

"Listen, man," Prometheus said, looking up at me, "I don't need that crap, just 'cuz you got a bad-hair day or somethin'."

"Sorry," I said, and I meant it. "It's just that I blew a baseball game after lunch and it's got me down."

"Happens."

"Yeah, happens. So how about you read some and I'll help you if you get stuck on a word?" I said.

"That's too slow. I can't *get* it, you know. The story don't stick in my head," Prometheus told me.

"Okay, so how about I read some, and then you read some and then we talk. Okay?"

"Yeah. And I gotta do three questions at the end, Ms. Noble say. And one more journal. You got time for all that?"

"I got an hour," I said, and began reading. "'Without, the night was cold and wet, but in the small parlor of Lakesnam Villa the blinds were drawn and the fire burned brightly. Father and son were at chess, the former, who possessed ideas about the game involving radical changes, putting his king into such sharp and unnecessary perils that it even provoked comment from the white-haired old lady knitting placidly by the fire.'" I looked up at Prometheus. "You understand all that?"

"No. You?"

"Kind of," I said. There wasn't enough time to talk about chess theories or the fact that houses in England often had names. None of that was very vital to the story anyway. "You just have to picture it," I said. "The family sitting around the fire, the father and son playing chess."

"Got it." Prometheus nodded.

"'Hark at the wind . . .'" I went on, groaning to myself. No wonder Prometheus couldn't read this. I kept thinking I should stop every sentence to explain words and phrases like *fakir* and *rubicund of visage*, but Prometheus would rather I just kept on with the story. At the end, with Herbert White's corpse knocking on the door, it actually gets quite exciting, regardless of vocabulary. I kept reading right up to the last paragraph, and stopped.

"Okay," I said, "I've read the whole thing except the end. "Your turn."

"Just finish it, man."

"C'mon, Pro. You said you'd read some. There's only four sentences to go, let's hear you do them."

He shot me a look full of what I took to be scorn, then bent over the book.

"'The k . . . knocking seized —'"

"Ceased," I interrupted.

"Yeah, ceased. 'The knocking ceased . . . suddenly,'" Pro took a deep breath, 'all . . . although the etch . . . ech . . . ' what?"

"Echoes."

"Right. 'The echoes of it were still in the house. He heard the chair . . . draw . . . drawn back and the door open. A cold wind r-rushed up the . . . staircase, and a long, loud . . . ' what's that?"

"'Wail of disappointment and misery.'"

"Right. 'From his wife gave him coo-courage to run down to her side, and then to the gate beyond. The street lamp fli-fli-fli . . . '"

"'Flickering opposite.'"

"Yeah. Doing that. 'Shone on a quiet and dee-deserted road.' The end." He let out his breath, as if he'd been holding it all the time he was reading.

"That's great, Pro," I said as enthusiastically as I could.

"No, man, that's lousy. If I could read great, you wouldn't have to be here and it wouldn't take me no five minutes to read four sentences." Pro leaned back in his chair.

"Okay, but you're going to get better," I said confidently.

"Sure, man. Just like you gonna play baseball for the Blue Jays."

Chapter 4

Journal. Sep 18

That Moonkid guy from high school showed up today ~~agin~~ again. Today he helped me read a story. The story was The Monkeys Paw and it was stupid. Lots of words didn't make no sense. Moonkid had to ~~exp~~ tell me what they mean. Like ~~sargan~~ sergeant-major was a guy in the army in the old days. A monkey's paw be like a rabbits foot, with luck and all that.

At the end, the old lady wants to let her kid in the house, but the kid be all ~~mut~~ mutilated** from a machine. So the old man makes a wish and the kid dispeard Bet lots of dads wishted they could make kids ~~dispear~~ disappear like that.

The story was sposed to be scary, but not for me.

I just think its kind of stupid. No such thing as monkeys paw that give you three wishes. Nothing gives you wishes but yoursself.

** see Ms. Noble, I lerned a new word. Mutilated. The old man mutilated the kid's face. How you like that?

Chapter 5

"You know what I don't get?" I said at supper that night.

"Probably plenty," Libby snapped back. She was playing with the stir-fried vegetables and rice on her plate like a two year old dawdling over a meal of strained peas.

I ignored her. I was in the middle of explaining about my tutoring session with Prometheus. "What I don't get is how a smart kid like Pro never learned how to read. I mean, he can read a little, like the average third-grader, but he's in grade seven now. So how did it happen?"

"Social factors," my father mumbled, his mouth full of rice. Sitting at the end of the table with his long hair untied, he looked like Jesus at the Last Supper. Except, of course, that he was missing the halo and at least ten of the twelve disciples.

"Rick, you *always* blame society," Libby piped up. "Did you ever stop to think about individual responsibility?"

My father smiled. "So you want to blame the problems of the schools on the kids who go there, eh?"

"I'm not saying that," Libby replied. "I'm not even talking about this particular kid, what's his name, Promiscuous or something?"

"Prometheus," I said, suddenly furious at her. "You're the one working on promiscuous, aren't you?"

"Ian, shut up," she said. Then she turned to my father, "Dad . . . "

"Okay, Ian, that was tacky. We're trying to be civilized, remember," my father said. As the Moonkid and Liberty wars have escalated, he finds himself more and more in the middle, like some kind of United Nations peacekeeper. And about as successful.

There was a pause while both Libby and my father stared at me, as if I should apologize for insulting Libby when she could freely insult Prometheus. Well, I wouldn't, and she better not. Libby may pretend to be savvy and sophisticated, but I know for a fact that she still sleeps with a ratty stuffed bear named Muffin, a fact I would not hesitate to use if necessary.

It wasn't. My father came in to smooth things

over. "Anyway, I think Prometheus is a victim of a racist society. He's black, poor, inner-city. If he were white, living in the suburbs with two investment banker parents, well, the kid would have had tutors and special programs since he was five years old. But as it is, all he's got is you, Ian."

"Trouble is, I don't really know what I'm doing," I said. "They stick the two of us in a room, and I read and he tries to read and then I fix up the spelling in his journal. Is that going to make any difference?"

"Not unless the kid wants it to make a difference," Libby said, her tone a little less angry. "All you do-good social workers and welfare workers and volunteers in the world aren't going to make any difference unless the kid wants to change things." She paused and stared at me. "Does he?"

"I . . . I don't know," I said. We really hadn't talked about that.

"I think I'd find out before I threw away every other afternoon on tutoring the kid," she said, looking at me as if my brains would fit nicely inside one of her lipstick cases. "There's other kinds of volunteer work, you know."

"Right," I snapped back. "Maybe I should volunteer to be a guide at the stock exchange, or polish the shoes of some poor Bay Street banker."

Libby just smiled at me. "Two good ideas, Ian. They'd both be good for you."

* * *

Prometheus and I were sent back to the library for our next tutoring session. I was in a better mood than last time; it was Prometheus who seemed upset. There was no smile, no bounce to his step, no patter as we walked down the hall. He pulled the green textbook from his book bag and thrust it in front of me.

"Can't read this crap," he muttered.

"Which crap?"

"This poem," he said, exaggerating the first syllable.

The textbook flopped open to page 224. "Because I could not stop for Death" by Emily Dickinson. Not one of my favorite poems, but not that awful either. I could see how it was supposed to tie into "The Monkey's Paw," part of some theme on death and the supernatural. But Ms. Noble's fondness for 19th century writers seemed a trifle strange on the cusp of the 21st century.

"It's not that bad," I said. "How about we read it and we trade lines. I'll do the first one and you do the second, like that. Okay?"

Prometheus just glared at me.

"'Because I could not stop for Death . . .'" I began. There was a long pause while Prometheus just sat there. "C'mon, you can do it. There are no tough words there. And I'll do the fourth line, too. Please?"

Prometheus mumbled the words. "'He kind-ly stopped for me.'" Then he looked up at me. "Who is this guy, anyhow? What she talking about?"

"The guy is Death," I explained. "It's like a metaphor —" I stopped when I saw the blank look in his eyes. "You ever heard about the Grim Reaper, you know, this guy dressed all in black with the big sickle who carries you away when you die? You've seen him in cartoons, right?"

"Yeah, I seen him."

"Well, it's like that. The idea of death is pretty scary, so people have kind of made up pictures of death to make it more human, sort of easier to understand. Ghosts are like that, goblins — the Grim Reaper."

"Death ain't so scary," Prometheus said.

"That's kind of what this poem is saying. Death is like this guy who shows up in a limo and takes you on a ride." I cringed at the simplification. Emily Dickinson would probably be rolling over in her grave if she'd heard. "Listen — 'The carriage held but just ourselves / And Immortality.' That means eternal life. Anyway, the two of them are in this carriage —"

"Like a hearse."

"Yeah, like a hearse. And off they go on a ride that will last forever. Now how about you do the next couple lines?"

Prometheus stared at the page. "'We slowly drove, he knew no haste, / And I had put away / My labor, and my . . . ' what?"

"'My labor, and my leisure too, / For his civility.'

Civility is like being nice to somebody. See, Death is being real nice to her, kind of like a boyfriend or a lover."

Prometheus smiled for the first time. "That's weird. She's one kinky lady."

I nodded. "Yeah, she was. Emily Dickinson lived alone her whole life, a kind of frustrated woman, you know? So her poems have got a lot of pent-up sex in them."

He raised one eyebrow. "There's sex in here?"

"Well, kind of. You know, the author and Death in this carriage, he's all polite and nice, maybe like the boyfriend Emily Dickinson never had."

"How come Ms. Noble didn't talk about all that?"

"Maybe she thinks you're too young?" I suggested.

"Plenty old enough to know about *that*," Prometheus said.

So we worked our way through the rest of the poem. I tried to make sense out of the symbolic tombstones later on, and the strange tone of the last stanza. With a little help on words like *cornice* (that we both had to look up, just to be sure), the poem gradually made sense. Then Prometheus tackled the three questions Ms. Noble had assigned, though I'm not sure what she's going to think of the answers.

I guess Libby's question was on my mind as Prometheus was writing in his notebook. What was I doing here? Was I just making life easier for Ms. Noble, filling in explanations of 'cornices' and 'sergeant-majors' so she could get her marking done on school time? What real difference did it make if Prometheus ever understood Emily Dickinson or her nineteenth-century sexual frustration? What was that going to do for him?

"Pro, you think this is a good idea?" I said before he started his journal.

"What? This poem? Goin' for a ride with Death?"

"No, this tutoring. You think it's helping you any?"

"Maybe. We only done it three times. You gonna back out already? Had a Big Brother once who did that. Took me to a couple ball games, then his wife had a kid and I was history. I seen that kind of thing before."

I shook my head, embarrassed. "No, not like that. I'm not quitting. I just wondered if you really want to read better, you know? Is it really important to you?"

"You think I want to be stupid my whole life?" Prometheus stared at me. "You think I like it when somebody gives you a part in a play and you can't even read it and everybody laughs at you?"

"I guess not," I said.

"So you just answered your own question," he said, smiling. "You know, Moonkid, sometimes I don' think you're all that smart."

Chapter 6

Journal. Sep 20

*Moonkid says I was in a rotten mood today.
Maybe true. I had a little trouble last night 'cause
my sister and my old lady started going at it, so
didn't get much sleep. Then Ms. Noble make us
read this poem, and it didn't make ~~no~~ any sense.
Moonkid help me figure out the poem be all about
sex. This horny old lady who ~~rote~~ wrote it thought
that death was some kind of loverboy. Pretty mean
loverboy, if you ask me, but I guess there's a lot of
them around.*

    *Now I ~~dont~~ don't know what I ~~spoced~~ am sup-
posed to write about. Moonkid say I ~~shuld~~ should
write about my family. Not much to say about
them. I got a mom, she works in a hospital and a
little brother Amos, and a sister, she don't live at*

*home. My old man be dead. Okay, he oughta be
dead. I had a stepdad, but he long gone, and a big
brother, but he took off, and a dog, but he ~~hadda~~
had to go to the country because he bark too much.
I really loved that dog. I loved him better than anybody else in my family ~~cept~~ except Amos and he's
a real jerk sometimes. I got uncles and ~~ante~~ aunts
but who cares? Wisht I had a dog again.*

*Anyhow, thats enough for today, Ms. Noble. No
big words, sorry. Okay, here's one. My house don't
have a cornice. How you like that?*

Chapter 7

That weekend, a peace offering from Libby appeared on my desk. I didn't see it at first, mixed in with the usual mess. In one corner were the school announcements, scraps of paper with interesting facts (*The ancient Greek poet Aeschylus died when an eagle mistook his bald head for a rock and dropped a tortoise on it to break the shell*), and copies of *Omni* and *The Smithsonian*. In the other corner were two particularly excellent Sunshinegirls ("Rosalie likes to suntan at the boardwalk and is knitting an afghan for her mother"), an old history project and a postcard from my mother ("Puerto Vallarta is wonderful, Ian. You should have come with us"). In the middle, on top of the *Edmund Scientific Catalog*, and a star map of South America, Libby had left a university library copy of *Tutoring Remedial Readers* by Harcrest and Whyte. For about a nanosecond, I was touched.

I opened the book and tried to find something that might help Prometheus, but it was heavy going. What's amazing for a book about remedial reading is that it's virtually unreadable itself: "It is imperative that classroom teachers familiarize themselves with the scope and sequence of reading skill development in order to successfully identify and diagnose students with incipient reading difficulties who might profit from a specific program of remediation, as distinct from those students suffering more general disabilities for whom such efforts will be merely palliative." Obviously nobody with reading problems is going to breeze through anything by Harcrest and Whyte.

Nor did the book offer that many practical ideas. Prometheus didn't seem to be dyslexic in any specific way. He didn't regularly reverse letters, or skip words, or guess at words he didn't know. Maybe he was a 'reluctant reader,' but he didn't spend his time with me yawning or staring out the window. As far as I could see, Prometheus just had trouble reading nineteenth-century writing filled with vocabulary he had never heard and ideas he had never thought of. Harcrest and Whyte called this a 'cultural deficit,' as if culture were some kind of bank and Prometheus either hadn't deposited enough or had somehow overdrawn his account. Their suggestion, logically, was 'cultural enrichment,' pumping those cultural pennies into Prometheus' account through "outings, discussion and other stimulating activities." That seemed like not a bad approach to me.

I made a couple of phone calls, one to my father, another to my grandmother, and managed to create the McNaughton Fund for Cultural Enrichment, a non-tax-deductible charity with exactly two contributors and one primary recipient. Now, just in case you think we're talking the Rockefeller Foundation here, let me point out that the McNaughton Fund assets totalled all of fifty dollars and the promise of a forty percent discount at my dad's bookstore, but it was a start. One more phone call to the planetarium got me the group rate (for a group of two) and reserved seats for Saturday afternoon.

So naturally I was smiling the next time I saw Prometheus. I had information. I had a plan. I had goodies to give out.

"What you grinnin' about, Moonkid?" Prometheus started off, slumping onto the couch.

"I've got some good stuff to tell you about," I said.

"Well, save it, man, 'cuz I got a pile of —" He looked around the library to make sure nobody was listening, then concluded with the obvious. "Listen, you know how to write good, don't you? You got all that kind of talk that the courts like to hear, right?"

"What courts?" I said, my smile fading. "You get in trouble with the cops?"

"Man, I'm always in trouble with the cops. But this time, it's not me. It's . . . " There was a pause. " . . . my friend."

"Your friend?" I repeated after him.

"Well, really his mom. He's got to write this letter to the court to tell 'em what happened."

I nodded. "An affidavit."

"Affi-who?" Prometheus replied, looking at me. "I said, you gotta write a *letter*."

"An affidavit is like a formal letter. You have to swear to it, like the kind of statement they use in court."

"Right," Prometheus said, clueing in. "So I said to him, I said I'd get you to help. You can do that, can't you?"

"I guess. You want me to fix the spelling and grammar, like I do on your journals?"

"No, man. I want you to *write* it. Then the guy can just copy it over like it be his own."

"So how do I know what to say?" I asked, a bit confused by all this. I'd done my own court affidavits often enough back in the days when my dad would get busted for various drug misdemeanors. And I was ready to go to court when they charged my dad with selling pornography that wasn't really pornographic, but nobody wanted my views on censorship. None of this qualified me as a lawyer, but it gave me a little familiarity with the courts.

"Listen, Moonkid, and I'll just tell ya. Here's some paper. Now you write, okay?" Along with the tough talk was a kind of little-kid look, as if Pro's words were masking the desperate fear that I might actually say no.

"Okay, have the kid put his address and the date — I'll put today, up here — and then the place where it's going, over here." *Ontario Court of Justice*, I wrote. "Criminal Division?" I asked before writing the words out. "Is it serious?"

"I guess. She got charged with assault," Prometheus replied.

Criminal Division, I wrote. "Okay, now what?"

Prometheus looked at me, then looked away as he thought. "Like this, only in fancy words, you know? I want to say that my mother didn't really mean to hit that kid, only talk to him 'cuz he was mouthing off and he deserved it. Oh, yeah, but it's not my mother, you know, it's this guy's. His name is Joe."

"Whoa," I said, trying not to smile at the mythical Joe. "How about we go a little slower? Usually you start with the facts — the date, the location, what happened. Then you make your big point at the end."

"Okay, okay," he replied quickly. "We was — Joe and his mom and his sister was walking down River Street, when was it, Thursday afternoon."

I started writing. "September nineteenth?"

"Yeah. And these three kids started mouthing

off to them. They was saying nasty stuff about the sister and all that."

"Provocation," I said as I wrote. "Do you know the names of the kids?"

"Zed, he's one, Johnny Boy be another. Some Vietnamese kid, he was there too."

"Maybe your friend Joe will know," I said, joining in on the hoax, "so I'll leave a blank."

"So these guys start mouthin' off and the mother, you know, she tries to pay no 'tention and just keep on going. But the kids be running along beside 'em, and yelling, and the sister, she starts to cry. And then a whole bunch of people start looking at 'em and laughing."

"Just give me a second to get that." There was a pause while I tried to phrase the language — *continuing taunts and provocations . . . social embarrassment*. "Okay."

"So the mother, she grabs this one kid, Johnny Boy, and gives him a spank. Just one, not even hard, to make him leave the sister alone. And the kid starts crying and screaming like she hit him with a brick or something. Anyway, the three little kids run away and the family goes shopping. But three hours later, the cops come to the door and say there's this complaint. So now the mom's gotta go to court 'cuz of child abuse or assault or something like that."

"The charge will never stand up," I said, sounding like one of the yuppie lawyers on *Street*

Legal. "So you want to finish up with a general statement that the spanking was reasonable under the circumstances, that the provoking kids were out of control and that the physical force has been exaggerated."

"Yeah, just like that," Prometheus said. "Except it's not for me, it's for Joe."

"Right," I said, finishing the letter. "Now you better read this back to me so you can read it to your friend Joe, so he knows what he supposedly wrote."

Prometheus grabbed the rough draft of the letter from my hands, then attacked each word with an effort I hadn't seen the week before in our attempts at W.W. Jacobs and Emily Dickinson. It's hard to imagine that a kid sounding out provocation can be positively heroic, but that's how it seemed to me. Real-life Prometheus fought his way through the language of the letter like mythical Prometheus battling side-by-side with Zeus. When the battle was over, he beamed at me.

"Thanks, Moonkid. I 'preciate it. Joe, he 'preciates it too."

"I'm sure," I said, trying to sound gracious. "Now, what does Ms. Noble want us to do today?"

"Don't know. We didn't read much in class the last couple days. She been doing more history and math. So I guess maybe we just do the journal," he said, simply enough. "Oh yeah, and she wants to see you after we get done."

"Oh, great," I said. I could hear the ominous chords in the background — dah-dah-dah-dum! — like Beethoven's Fifth with dark storm clouds rolling up on a movie screen. While it was *possible* that Ms. Noble simply wanted to praise me for my efforts and bring me up to date on her lesson plans, it seemed far more likely that I was going to be chewed up, mangled, bruised and *mutilated*, to use Prometheus' favorite word. But there was no point in sharing my fears with him. Best just to go ahead, I thought.

"How about we do a little reading first?" I suggested. "For practice."

"Read what?" he said. "I already read that letter, didn't I?"

"Yeah, but maybe we could read a little of whatever book you're reading at home."

"What book?" he asked.

"The book you're reading for yourself. You know, a novel or whatever. Don't you have to read something to do book reports?"

"Nope. Only have to read what Ms. Noble says. I don't read at home."

"Well, no wonder —" I began, before I shut down my own tongue. I almost spilled the simple truth: no wonder the kid couldn't read if the only time he ever did it was in school. "Pro, it's like this," I said, starting over, "if you want to read better, you've got to practice it every day. It's like playing piano —" *Lousy simile*, I said to myself.

" . . . or like playing baseball, you get better with practice."

"That why you so good at baseball?" he said, smiling at his own joke.

"That's why I'm so *bad* at it," I told him. My bad came out sounding almost like jive. "But I can live without playing baseball. You can't live a decent life without knowing how to read. You told me that yourself, Pro."

"Hey, man, ease up. You s'posed to be my tutor, not give me lectures from way up on some high horse, you know?" He looked down at the floor.

I felt embarrassed. "Sorry. You're right. You got anything in your house to read?"

"No way. My mom, she just read these trashy romance books. You know, *Purple Passion Romance*, that kind of stuff. I ain't gonna read that."

"Nothing else?" I asked. Why was I so incredulous? A lot of families would rather have their eyeballs instant-glued to the TV set, their evenings filled with two-dimensional characters and electronic laugh tracks, than shell out ten bucks for a book.

"Got a couple *Peanuts* books, you know, Charlie Brown and Lucy and those guys?" Prometheus said. "Got 'em from the school library in grade three and the teacher forgot, so I never took 'em back. I probably read those books a couple hundred times."

"That's it?" I said.

"That's it," he said.

"Okay, so next time I'll bring you some books," I said, coming up with another project for the McNaughton Fund. And then I remembered. I'd been so thrown by the letter and the image of Prometheus' book-empty apartment that I'd forgotten all about my plan. "And I've got an idea to solve the problem with your journal entries. You know how you're always saying you've got nothing to write about? Well, I thought that if we did something together, maybe we could read some books that go along with it and you'd have something to write about."

"Like what?"

"Like astronomy."

"The planets," Prometheus said, looking at me as if I'd lost my mind. "We're gonna go to outer space." His voice was full of scorn. "Ri-ight."

"No, the planetarium," I said quickly. "I've got two tickets to the Saturday afternoon show. I could come over, meet you about two, then we take the bus and see the show. You'd be home for supper."

"This for real?"

"For real. All paid for. What do you think?"

I could tell he was thinking hard. He looked away from me, at the floor, and his brow furrowed as he turned the idea over. It hadn't occurred to me that he might say no, that he wouldn't be grateful for the chance for a free afternoon at the planetarium. But a lot of things hadn't occurred to me before then.

"Nah," he said. Then he must have seen the look on my face. "I mean, thanks and all. But I'm gonna be busy."

"How about another day?" I said.

"Nah. It's not a good idea. You just bring me a book and I'll read that, okay?"

I sat there, stunned. For perhaps the first or second time in my life, I was at a dead loss for words.

"I better get this journal going," Prometheus said, avoiding my gaze. "Ms. Noble gonna think we didn't do nothin'."

I sat looking out the window as Prometheus wrote. It was three o'clock, fifteen minutes before the end of the school day. Down in the concrete playground, a grade three class was playing pickle-in-the-middle dodgeball. An overweight kid was in the middle, trying desperately to hit someone on the other team with the ball, but missing pathetically time after time. The level of the taunts and insults rose as each throw got worse. I felt for him, and looked away.

On the other side of the street were the Royal Home projects, a set of 1950's low-rise units that had been built on the site of a former slum, and quickly become a slum themselves. Most of the students at this school, including Prometheus, came from those projects. In a few minutes, the kids would walk across the street — avoiding junkies, dope-dealers, the odd prostitute, an array of homeless people and terminal alcoholics — and go back to a real life in the apartments and hallways of the projects. It was a real life I knew nothing about.

"Okay, I'm done," Pro said. It was 3:10.

I read through the text, showed him a couple of corrections, and Prometheus laboriously fixed his errors. When the bell rang, an audible cry of relief went up from the whole school.

"Thanks, man," Prometheus said, as he put away his journal notebook and got up to leave. He walked over to the library door, then stopped and turned back to me, his eyes still on the floor. "You done a lot for me today," he said quietly. "I 'preciate it."

"Sure thing," I muttered as he went out to the hall. "See you — " I was going to say Wednesday, but I wasn't so sure about that. I wasn't so sure that Ms. Noble was going to let me see Prometheus ever again.

* * *

She entered *enormously*. I once saw a TV special where the opera singer Jessye Norman came out onto the stage at Carnegie Hall in New York, and the same adverb came to mind then. Entering *enormously* involves more than just physical size. It is a particular kind of slow, elegant movement that only a very large and powerful person can accomplish. There is a certain sense of style, of breeding, of overwhelming certainty that can be communicated by a step or two and the mere sweep of an arm. I was, to say the least, impressed.

"Young man," she said, making no effort to smile at me.

"Ian," I reminded her. If this was to be a chewing out, at least the chewee should have a name in the mind of the chewer.

"Ian, I asked to speak to you because I have some concerns about how your tutoring sessions with Prometheus are going. Please sit down."

I hadn't realized that I was standing. Perhaps it was unconscious, the rising to one's feet in the presence of nobility. Ms. Noble herself did not take a seat. She looked down upon me the way a queen might look upon kneeling subjects.

"I had a chance to read through Prometheus' journal and some of his reading response questions, and I must say that there is a real improvement. His answers are longer and more detailed and his journal entries, well, at least there are journal entries. I can see you've also been helping him with some of the spelling."

"Yes'm," I said. There was that expression again.

"But the *content* causes me some concern. Your

interpretation of the Emily Dickinson poem, for instance. I *assume* it was your interpretation."

I think it's fascinating the way some people can bring their entire weight, all three hundred pounds or so, to rest on one or two words like *content* and *assume*.

"Yes'm," I repeated myself.

"Well, it struck me as a bit crude, Ian, and probably quite inappropriate for a student like Prometheus in grade seven. 'Because I could not stop for Death' is not about sex."

"No, ma'am. But there is a kind of sexual undertone. There's a fair amount of Freudian symbolism I didn't even get into —"

"And I'm glad you didn't," she said, cutting me off. "This is not a rich, suburban high school, and these are not gifted students. It is a major achievement getting them to read poetry at all."

"But, if —"

She cut me off again. "No 'buts,' young man."

"Ian," I blurted out. "I have a name."

We glared at each other. She might outweigh me by two hundred pounds and be standing way over my head, but I still have a very resolute stare. I can stare down three-year-olds in strollers, five-year-olds who think I look weird and eight-year-olds who think they have the concentration to win a bet-you'll-blink-before-I-do contest. But I could not out-stare Ms. Noble.

"Ian," she said, not blinking even once, "I think

it's important that we understand each other if this tutoring is to continue."

I blinked at the *if*. A quick image of Markdale High School flashed into my mind. I pictured Mrs. Greer, finger pointing, mouthing the word *go*. I shuddered. "Yes'm," I said, defeated.

"Your job is to augment what happens in class, not to undermine it." She looked out the window, a little smile on her face. "I do appreciate the way you've helped Prometheus with his writing and in answering questions, but it will do him no good in the long run if you corrupt his attitude towards school or undermine his respect for authority."

I should have said something. I should have talked about how Prometheus *already* felt about the cops. I should have explained that Prometheus probably knew more about sex than I did. I should have told her that *nobody* could ever undermine her authority. But I sat there, mute.

"So I would appreciate it if you would stick more closely to what we're doing in class and be . . . " She paused, probably for effect. " . . . a little less creative in how you approach the material. Prometheus likes you. He perhaps even respects you. So you must use your time here every other day to help him and not interfere with the rest of his program. Do you understand me, Ian?"

"Yes'm," I said, gulping. Why does spittle always get stuck in your throat on occasions like this?

"Good," she said, stretching out the o's. "Because I would certainly like to see the tutoring continue. It will be good for both of you."

Ohmygod, I screamed to myself, in the words of the more dimwitted segment of my generation. Ms. Noble, my sister and my father, the most unlikely trio on earth, all seize on the same expression. *It will be good for you.* Like cough syrup or a vitamin pill or something else that gets rammed down your throat thanks to the coercion of medical science.

I have news for them, I thought as I stumbled out of the school. So far, this has *not* been good for me. It's been depressing, and stupid, and a waste of my time. And as soon as I said all that to myself, I saw an image of Libby's mocking face. She couldn't be right, could she?

Chapter 8

Journal. Sep 23

I don't ~~got~~ have much to say today. The weekend was stupid, just like always. Guys in the ~~hood~~ neighborhood ~~was~~ were hassling me, so I rode my bike downtown again. A cop stop me and ask if it be really my bike. I said, "Sure, man. Is that really your ~~bage~~ badge?" Cops don't do nobody ~~no~~ any good. There never around when you need them. And they always stick ~~his~~ there nose in when you don't need them. Just ask my mom.

Sorry Ms. Noble, that's what I think. Thanks for reading my journals last week. And thanks for getting Moonkid to help me. He's ~~ok~~ OK. That's all for today.

Chapter 9

One of the many irrational aspects of earthlings is that they seem absolutely unable to recognize when they are most in need of help. If you approach a young kid in the playground, for instance, whose head is being pounded against the ground by some larger kid who treats the human skull like some ill-shaped basketball, and you say, "Would you like some help?" the beaten kid will invariably say, "No, it's fine. No problem." He will say this even as his teeth crunch together with the impact, even as his hair receives a gravel shampoo. He will say this despite any obvious unfairness in his assault or the abject impossibility of his triumphing without assistance.

I know this, of course, because the kid with the slightly dented skull has frequently been me.

But I digress. What's important to observe is the principle: those who most need help are least likely to admit it, even less likely to accept it when offered. The student struggling over the area of a parallelogram will chew his tongue, scratch his head, covertly glance at any answer paper in sight, but will never come out and admit, "I can't do this stupid thing." The nerd most desperate to pick up a girl whose bodacious attributes have made her the subject of universal male attention will hem, haw, hum and make a thorough fool out of himself before actually admitting, "I haven't got a chance with a girl like that." I know both of these examples to be true, of course, because the idiot or nerd in question often happens to be me. And I would never, ever admit that to anyone else. I have publicly rejected help, assistance, advice, comfort — I have literally wallowed in the mud of my own proud incompetence — rather than admit any of my many deficiencies.

So why was I surprised that Prometheus behaved just like me? Why was I so depressed that even my utterly insensitive sister could sense it?

"What's the matter, Ian?" she said on Wednesday morning. "You get some direful message from the inhabitants of your planet? Sunspots on Alpha Centauri? What?" She was being unusually witty so early in the morning, a sharp contrast to her usual breakfast pose of weary urban sophisticate.

"Nothing," I said, preposterously.

"That book I got for you help any?" she went on.

"A bit," I said. "It showed me a lot of things that don't work."

"Well, cheer up, Ian. You and your do-good comrades will find something that does work sometime in the next thousand years or so. In the meanwhile, the sun is shining, the blue jays are singing —"

"Blue jays don't sing, Libby. They squawk. And why are you so ridiculously cheerful at an hour when any sensible person is moping and rubbing sleep out of his eyes?"

She gave me a rather imperious look, not on the same level as Ms. Noble's, but still quite impressive. "You think I'm stupid enough to tell you — and have your sarcasm drag me down to your bargain basement of despair? No way, José. I'll tell you some other day." And with that little rhyme she performed a clumsy pirouette that showed just how much physical agility all the McNaughtons have been gifted with, and went off to the bathroom.

I trudged to school and managed to avoid staring too hard at the gaggle of gorgeous women clustered near Jessica Smith-Weir's locker. Then I discovered that I had left my biology notebook at home and that a piece of apple left in my locker two weeks previously had managed both to attract mice and develop a rather fuzzy mold. It was not an auspicious start to the day.

In biology, we watched a video on algae which was just about as exciting as you can imagine. By the time it was finished, there was audible snoring from at least two individuals in the room, only one of whom was our teacher. This was not really a problem. The class that came next was the problem. Math. Incalculably dreadful math.

Mathematics in my school used to come in three varieties, designated at the grade ten level as Math 2E, 2A and 2B. According to Libby, who was a product of this system, E stood for Eager beaver, A for All the other normal kids and B for Bumbling, blithering idiots.

Under the old system, I would never have made it into Math 2E with the brainers and sophisticates — those kids with trendy Ralph Lauren glasses who carry three-thousand-dollar notebook computers, and wonder why everyone else doesn't. But I would have been pleasantly ensconced in Math 2A with the normal assortment of high school jocks, beauty queens, punkers and macho men — kids who dress entirely in black and kids whose clothes cost as much as my father's car; kids who use dental floss daily and those who shower but once a week; kids who have seen *Ferris Bueler's Day Off* twenty times and those who still watch *Wheel of Fortune*. And I would have had little contact with the kids in Math 2B, who find the area of a square a difficult concept and the area of a triangle a brain-teaser.

But just last year a liberal reform came to our school's math department: destreaming. While the Es managed to keep their special class (they're gifted, you know), the As and Bs got tossed together. The theory was that the As would help the Bs, or the Bs would learn from the As, or that whatever worked in primary school would continue to operate through to university. Perhaps such a system even works in some jurisdictions, or with computers that really do toss together the As and Bs like a chef tossing the lettuce in a salad. But it does not work in *this* system with our computer. My destreamed math class, Math 2001C, is almost entirely made up of the arithmetically lame and halt. People who will never balance their checkbooks or even think of looking over their credit card statements. People who will have to pay H&R Block to do their income tax. And so on.

Now I may not be a mathematical genius — in fact, my math skills have always been quite humble compared to my obvious talents in language and science — but surely the computer made some mistake in creating class 2001C. Surely I deserve better than this.

There are twenty students assigned to Math 2001C, two of whom have never appeared and may be entirely fictitious, one who has recently gone to a juvenile detention center, one who dropped out after getting proudly pregnant, and one who appears only once a week, apparently bouncing around between group homes and a kindly aunt in the suburbs.

The fifteen who show up more-or-less regularly consist of one good student, John Parton, who is at the guidance office on a daily basis trying to get transferred out, one average student, yours truly, and a collection of thirteen individuals who wear their mathematical stupidity as proudly as someone else might wear the Order of Canada.

At the top end of this group we have Shannon Wareham, who aspires to a career in hairdressing; Bronson Chamberlain, who deals a fair portion of the drugs at school; Chris Petrie who, at almost seven feet tall, could have a career in basketball but is so uncoordinated that he frequently appears bandaged from collisions with door frames and parked cars; and Sara Shaker, who seems to spend an inordinate amount of time arranging, rearranging, coloring and recoloring her hair.

At the bottom end, we have students like Ronnie Conner who has real difficulty tying his shoes, and most days is quite unaware that his shirt is mis-buttoned or his hair is sticking out at odd angles.

I tend to prefer the students at the bottom end, who are invariably cheerful, over those at the top, who can be surly or dangerous.

Presiding over this assemblage is Mr. Swayze, the teacher, who is famous around the school for his two hundred identical Harris Tweed sport coats, all with leather elbow patches, and for the unusual amount of hair growing out of his nostrils and ears. Mr. Swayze makes no effort to disguise his disgust at destreaming, and his general view that our class is an educational atrocity. Ordinarily he keeps us busy with the 'independent progress' approach to math, which means we sit in our seats and sweat through one of the many different-colored workbooks he has arrayed near the chalkboard. The reward for having completed the red level is to be allowed to go on to the blue level, followed by the purple level, the green level, the orange level — a veritable rainbow of levels that must, I suppose, finish with dazzling white and the meaning of $E=mc^2$. But on this particular day, Mr. Swayze decided to become creative and attempt a lesson.

"Okay, are you listening?" he began, waiting for the din to drop a bit. "No workbooks today." There was a mix of groans and cheers. "We're going to form into problem-solving groups."

The class was stunned. We had never before been in groups. Only rarely did we even work as a class. No one was quite sure what Mr. Swayze had mixed into his breakfast cereal.

"I want you to organize yourselves into four groups. There are fifteen of you, so about how many people will be in each group?" There was a pause while he searched the room for a victim. "John?"

Attention focused on John Dunstable, a lanky boy who seems to have spent most of his childhood on an Alberta horse farm and only occasionally in a school. "Uh, six?"

"Fifteen, into four groups," repeated Mr. Swayze. "Four goes into fifteen . . . "

"Three!" John shouted, beaming. "With some left over."

"Right," agreed Mr. Swayze, resisting, I'm sure, the temptation to slap his head. "So you'll be in groups of three or four, got it? Now move your desks and let me see these groups."

There was a noisy shifting of desks, some quick negotiation and altercation as students manoeuvred around the room like kids driving bumper-cars at the amusement park. Finally, there were two groups of three, two groups of two, one group of four and me over in the corner.

"I said *four groups*" Mr. Swayze yelled, a look of disgust on his face. "Try again."

Beneath his stern gaze, the class began to move again. Bronson ejected John Dunstable from his group of five; the two groups of two combined into one. This left John and I looking for a place.

I've never been able to understand how some people can automatically fit into groups while others of us are always on the outside, or last-in. You'd think that my fellow students would realize the valuable contribution I could make to their group, if not with my math skills, with my wit and general good humor. But as I moved towards Bronson's group, I got a quick, "Not you," of dismissal. Then I turned towards Sara Shaker and the girls, but found their backs to me and a general refusal to acknowledge my existence. Finally, I turned to Ronnie Conner's group, but John Dunstable had already made this a foursome.

"Looks like everybody's in a group but you, Ian," Mr. Swayze said. I thought it was charming of him to point this out to the whole class. "Chris," he said, authoritatively, "Ian will be in your group."

"Do we have to take him, Mr. Swayze?" Chris whined, a funny sound from a seven-foot-tall student.

"Yes, you have to."

There was a groan from the group and laughter from the others who had been spared the social embarrassment of my presence. I moved my desk over towards the gigantic figure of Chris, but found his little cluster of three none too accommodating. I pushed my desk in; they moved their desks away. Chris stared at me like I was a crawling insect to which he would ordinarily apply a squirt of Raid. The other two had expressions on their faces as if my deodorant had failed. My F&I index soared as the embarrassment increased. All this, and the lesson hadn't even begun.

* * *

"You down in the dumps again?" Prometheus greeted me.

"Yeah," I said honestly. I had been sitting in the library, staring at my hands, wondering why I had ever been born, or sent to this planet, or otherwise made subject to ostracism, castigation and social — to use Prometheus' newfound word — mutilation.

"Well, cheer up, man. I brought something for you." Prometheus had the big grin on his face, the kind of grin that showed his pointed back teeth.

"Yeah?"

"Yeah, it's in here." He reached in his backpack and brought out a paperback book: *You Can't Win Them All, Charlie Brown*. "For you, Moonkid. If you want to give me one of your books, I'm gonna give you one of mine. Fair's fair."

I took the dog-eared paperback, handling it like a treasure. The pages were yellowed, the seventy-five cent corner price gave me the vintage, but it was Prometheus' smile that gave the book its value. I was, as humans say, touched.

"Thanks, man," I said, and smiled myself.

"Now what you got for me? You didn't forget, did you?" There was a mix in his voice of expectation, and fear of disappointment.

"Got it right here," I said. I felt my earlier troubles lifting, like a smothering comforter pulled off a feverish child. "It's called *Rumblefish*."

"What's that mean?" Pro asked, taking the

black-covered paperback from me.

"Well, it means two things, really. There are these fighting tropical fish called Bettas. If you put two of them together in a tank, they tear each other apart. It's sort of like street gangs, that kind of senseless fighting. So the book is about gang stuff and how this guy, Rusty James, gets over being a rumblefish."

I thought that wasn't a bad explanation. It wasn't at the level of a librarian's book talk, but I've never had aspirations to be a librarian, or much of anything, if the truth were told. I've spent too much of my life worrying about getting back to my home planet, and not enough thinking about my future here on earth.

"So there's a message, eh?"

"Yeah. A lot of books have a message, and I guess this one does, too."

Prometheus had opened the book, looking warily at the text. I had already checked it out thanks to formulas in *Tutoring Remedial Readers*: readability level 4.5 to 5.1, easy enough for Pro to handle on his own.

"I'm not in a gang, you know," he said.

"Well, neither am I, but I still thought it was a good book. Want me to start it off for you?"

"Later, man. First we gotta get some questions done. Ms. Noble gave us a new story today, something called 'The Pit and . . . ' and the something."

"'The Pit and the Pendulum.'" I wondered how

many more wordy horror stories Ms. Noble intended to inflict on the class.

"Yeah, that's it," Pro said, smiling at my recognition.

"So you probably need me to read it again, don't you?" I offered.

"No way, man. She played this tape — it was real good — and I could follow along, mostly. I think I got the story pretty good. But she didn't give us 'nough time for the questions. So we gotta do questions and then the journal, okay?"

"Okay," I nodded.

"And I got some news for you. About that astrology thing."

"The planetarium?"

"Yeah, that's it. I checked with my mom and she said it's okay if I go with you. I got a couple bucks to pay my way in."

I was astonished. I guess I'd given up so thoroughly on the idea of cultural enrichment excursions that it didn't occur to me Prometheus might change his mind.

"So you can go?"

"That's what I said, man. You know, you gotta learn how to listen up a little better."

"That's great," I said, smiling so widely that my cheeks hurt. "But you don't need to bring money. I can take care of both of us."

A sudden dark look came over Prometheus' face. "What you think I am, a charity case?" He stared at me, his eyes wide, the whites tinted slightly yellow. "Nobody in my family ever took charity, never been on welfare, neither. Gibbses look after our own, you understand?"

"Sorry, I just —"

He cut off my apology. "It's okay, s'long as you understand. I pay my own way and we'll have a real good time. Trip'll probably give me enough stuff to fill my journal up for a month, you think?"

"Yeah, probably."

"So let's get these dumb questions done. I want to read a bit of that rumble book 'fore we got to go. Okay?"

Sure it was okay. Prometheus took out his notebook, stuck his tongue firmly in the corner of his mouth and began writing an answer to question one. I watched him for a while, then listened to the birds outside the library window. The pigeons were making their usual cooing and scrabbling sounds, but there must have been a blue jay out there too. And he was — to the extent that blue jays can do so — trying to sing.

Chapter 10

I gave Moonkid one of my books today. It's called You Cant Win Them All, Charlie Brown. *It's really a bunch of* ~~ponut peanut~~ *Peanuts* ~~cartons~~ *cartoons. I like it because it's funny. It's not all that easy to read, eather. There's big words like clastrophobia and melancholy,* ~~specilly~~ *especially when Lucy and her little brother Linus talk.*

There's a lot of funny cartoons in there. Moonkid likes the one where Snoopy is going to read this book called War and Peace. *Linus comes up and says, "You're only going to read one word a day?" and Snoopy say "Why not? I'm in no hurry . . . besides, I like to think about what I read."*

That really broke Moonkid up, and me too. I didn't know that War *and* Peace *was a real long book, either. Moonkid says it* ~~be~~ *is 1200 pages long. I figured it out. If you read one page a day, it would take 3 years, 3 months and 11 days to finish the book. If you read one word a day, it would take you 1344 years to finish the book. Guess* ~~that be~~ *that's a little too slow.*

I learned a new word from Moonkid today. Hilarious. The comics is hilarious. Sometimes Moonkid is hilarious. I wish sometimes you were hilarious, Ms. Noble. I guess teachers ~~ain't~~ *are not supposed to be.*

I have to go. Moonkid gave me a new book to read. It's called Rumblefish *and I guess it's about gangs. The cover looks pretty good anyhow.*

Chapter 11

Prometheus was already outside the planetarium when I arrived. He was leaning against the concrete wall, dressed in his best baggy rapper clothes, his oversized Converse running shoes an outrageous white in contrast to the rest of his black and red outfit. He was frowning from the sunshine, busy looking up and down the street as I walked up.

Amid the crowd of little white kids waiting for the show, yuppie shoppers on their way to Yorkville, and university students taking Saturday off, Prometheus looked as out of place as Ice-T at a symphony concert. Then again, dressed in my grunge clothes and sporting a stupid grin, I didn't fit in all that well, either.

"Been waiting long?" I began.

"Little bit," he said, not venturing a grin. "Wanted to be sure I got here in plenty time, you know? Good thing you showed up. Otherwise, those cops over there gonna charge me with loitering."

I followed his gaze to where the police were standing, apparently doing nothing more than enjoying the sunshine.

"Isn't that a little paranoid?" I asked him, then saw the blank look on his face. "I mean, what makes you think they're after you?"

Prometheus just looked at me. "I been hanging around here for 'bout an hour. Those two been hanging around for 'bout that long too. It ain't like neither of us got nothin' better to do, you know what I mean?"

I decided to change the subject. One man's paranoia is another man's reasonable expectation of disaster, I always say. My father, for instance, spent the first part of his life anticipating harassment from almost everyone. But this was when he was actually being busted by the police on a regular basis, and hassled by everything from dogs to teenagers with spray paint cans and rocks. Thus my father did not suffer paranoia. He was merely aware of the kind of treatment the world hands out to ex-hippie, commie-pinko-druggie guys with long hair-not-tied-in-a-ponytail who are otherwise minding their own business. I can only imagine what it's like when people go beyond objecting to your ideas or your hair, and pick on you just because your skin happens to be black.

"You buy your ticket yet?" I asked Pro.

"No, man. I was waitin' for you. No way I was going in this place by myself. Here." He handed me four dollars, the student fare posted on the sign, and I handed him a loony back.

"What's this?" he said, looking at the loony like I had spit in his hand.

"I got us a deal, remember?"

"Oh, yeah," he said, smiling again. "What's that you guys say, 'a buck saved is a buck earned'?"

I nodded. "Used to be a penny, but that was before inflation. Come on, it's time."

We got in line heading to the ticket booth, finally reaching the front only to be greeted with the usual hassle about "group rates?" and "how do you spell your name?" Then we bypassed the color slides of comets and 3-D diagrams of the solar system to go right into the theater.

"Hey, man, how you like these seats?" Prometheus said to me. It had taken him all of two seconds to figure out that the seats tilted back like the Lay-Z-Boys you can buy through the Home Shopping Channel.

"Comfy," I said.

"What's that thing in the middle there?"

"The projector?"

"Yeah," Pro said, straightening his chair to look around. "What you call it? I gotta know so I can write up my journal, right?"

"Yeah. It's called a Zeiss Genastar projector," I said. I'd been here often enough to get most of the information down pat. "It's going to fill the whole ceiling up there with stars."

"Kinda like God." Pro tilted the chair back again.

"Kind of like German optics," I said. "It projects the whole universe up there — and it moves, so you can get the night sky at different seasons, and different places."

"The sky moves around?" Pro said, skeptically.

"Yeah, didn't you ever notice? The planets move, the earth rotates, some stars pulsate. When you see the show, you'll see that the whole universe is in motion. It's beautiful, really."

"Went up to the top of our building once," Pro said, "and looked at the stars up there. But didn't see 'em move."

"You just didn't look long enough. If you spent the whole night — Wait, the show's starting."

There was an explosion of music from one side, a subtle darkening of the theater, more heavy-duty symphonic music to shut up the jabbering little kids, and then the show began. The title was *Fire in the Sky*. The blurb outside had said it was about the "sun's influence on the earth, from the ice ages to the present day." While I'd seen half a dozen planetarium shows before this — always keeping an eye open for messages from whatever my home planet might be — *Fire in the Sky* was a new one for me and it was a first for Prometheus. I looked over at his face and saw him bug-eyed.

"Pretty good, eh?" I said. Twenty slide projectors threw up images of the horizon of downtown Montreal while the Zeiss projector filled the domed ceiling with stars.

"Yeah, man. This is something," he whispered back. "Never knew there was so many stars."

"You can't see them all from the city," I said.

"Never been outta the city," he said, and then the music welled up again.

At the edges of the dome, the city of Montreal fell into darkness while the announcer talked about how sunspots cause strange things to happen here on earth in their eleven-year cycles: power failures, weather changes, drought and famine, snow in June and stock market crashes in September. Then a huge image of the sun filled the dome, complete with sunspots and solar flares, the whole thing so bright I had to squint to look at it.

"What about other possible life in the universe?" the announcer asked. I resisted the temptation to raise my hand and let them know that I was already visiting. Besides, I wanted to see what he had to say on the issue. On the dome, there was a quick projection of how unique the earth was: the right orbit, the right size of sun, the right combination of water and atmosphere and carbon atoms to sustain life as we know it. But with 400 billion stars in the universe, chances were that at least a few of them had developed life forms, too. Which one do I come from? I wondered, just as the announcer began reviewing some possibilities: Alpha Centauri, the closest star; some part of the Crab Nebula, some part of the Cygnus constellation. But if there was life out there, the announcer concluded, it hadn't made any attempt to contact Earth.

Why would anybody want to? I thought. Why would any intelligent set of creatures out there in the Milky Way want to have anything to do with this tribe of warring, ill-mannered, sadistic and dangerous humans? The human species had already wiped out several hundred other species on the planet, taken over most of Earth's land mass like some out-of-control weed, and made every effort along the way to destroy itself. Any sensible alien would have observed this, and then set up communication with one of the more intelligent creatures on the planet — dolphins or porpoises or earthworms — avoiding humanity like the plague that it is. Or they would have sent an agent — like me — disguised as a human to report back on whether the species was making any progress.

Beam me up! I mumbled to the dome. *I'm ready to file my report.*

"What's that?" Prometheus asked.

"Uh, nothing," I said, embarrassed. No sense letting the kid know how weird I really was.

The planetarium show went on to some elementary school stuff — planetary rotation, the seasons, the water cycle, photosynthesis — and then came back to what people had been doing to the ozone layer. According to the announcer, the human species, with its automobiles and aerosol cans, has done more over the last fifty years to upset the relationship of the earth and the sun than all the other species since the age of the dinosaurs. At the rate human beings were going at it, they'd bring about another ice age in 13,000 years and wipe themselves off the face of the planet. Then the whole evolutionary cycle would have to start again, maybe this time forming a better species, one that wouldn't be quite so self-destructive.

Or maybe not.

"That was cool, Moonkid," Prometheus said as the lights came up.

"Gets you thinking," I said, honestly enough.

"I wanna see that machine up there. What you call it, a Zeus projector?"

"A Zeiss projector. Zeus was a Greek god. Zeiss is a German optical firm."

"I knew that," Prometheus said, grinning at me. And then he was zooming up to the front, faster than anybody who wears size-thirteen shoes has any right to move.

Prometheus stared open-mouthed at the projector, which loomed over his head like a giant, two-headed insect. He checked out the complex systems of gears and struts that supported it and allowed it to move, the large globes which hid perforated copper plates that projected light to form the Milky Way, the hundreds of lenses covering the globes and projecting images of planets and stars and the solar system. He was studying the whole thing from a variety of angles when the guy from the control panel came up beside me.

"Can I help you two?" he said, in a tone that meant *You kids better stop eyeballing this thing or I'll have the guards kick you out of here.*

Prometheus looked over at him with a smile on his face. It's the kind of smile that is sometimes called 'disarming,' because it's almost impossible not to smile back, even if you're not well-disposed towards curious kids. "Yeah, I got a couple questions. You're the guy that makes all this work, right?"

The guy puffed up a bit. "Well, mostly the show is automated, but they still need me to operate the projector because this baby is pretty old — almost forty years now. I was twelve when it was built."

"Really?" Prometheus said, as if the guy looked like he needed proof to get into a bar. "So you make this thing move and turn and all that?" Talk about buttering somebody up.

"That's right," the man said. "Would you like to see?" he asked.

I was amazed. Here was this old guy, who had

been ready to kick us out two minutes before, now smiling like a little kid about to show off his latest Lego construction. How had it turned around so fast — a couple of questions and a smile?

"Sure," Prometheus said. He followed the old guy back towards the control panel, and I dogged along behind them.

"This new show is almost all on the computer," the man told us. "I'm down to just these four cues." He held up a sheet of paper with some of the show dialogue written on it. "In the old days, we used to run everything from here. I'd do the narration with this microphone, and run the slide projectors with this set of buttons — there's two sets of twelve up around the edge there — and run the star projector with these controls. It was like a three-ring circus then, but it's almost too easy now. Of course, some day they'll figure out how to work the Genastar entirely by computer, and then I'll just sit here like an idiot watching the computer screen."

"Won't be much fun, will it?" Prometheus said sympathetically.

"Would you like to try out the controls?" the old guy asked him.

"Me? Could I?" Pro sounded just like a kid. On second thought, I guess he is a kid, even if he is bigger than me.

"Sure. Sit down here. Now if you hit that button, the lights will dim a bit, and that turns the projector on," he said, showing Pro where to press. The room grew darker and the dome filled with stars. "That's it. Now with the projector in its current position, you get the night sky in North America, and if you hit that button . . . "

Prometheus did, and the stars began to rotate around their axis. The effect made me dizzy.

"That's how the stars move during the course of one evening, because of the earth's rotation. Of course, if you hit that button, you get South America . . . "

Prometheus pressed and the Zeiss projector began to move, like some lumbering dinosaur looking for its prey. There was confusion as stars shone all over the room, and then another night sky appeared in the dome.

"October in Buenos Aires," the old guy said.

"Aaa-maazing," Prometheus said, and it truly was.

"Now if you kids would like to learn some more, the Astronomical Society has night classes here with telescopes, and sometimes using the projector. You can get a schedule out in front."

"That'd be great," Prometheus said, as the old guy brought up the house lights. "And thanks. Thanks for lettin' me use the machine."

"Glad to," said the man. "Nice to see some young people who are interested. Now if your friend would like to try . . . "

"Oh, that's okay," I said, trying to be mature

or blasé or something like that.

"It's cool," Prometheus said to me.

"Yeah, but it's okay. Another day," I told them both. I guess I felt left out, as if Prometheus and this guy had connected and I was still awaiting signals from Alpha Centauri.

Prometheus climbed down from the control booth and shook hands with the old man, offering an even wider smile and more thanks. Then the two of us left the theater and made our way down the stairs into the front foyer. Prometheus grabbed a pamphlet from the Astronomical Society with a schedule of classes. I frowned, waiting for my eyes to get adjusted to the bright daylight.

"C'mon, Moonkid. I'll buy you an ice cream," Prometheus said as we went out to the front steps. In front of us were street vendors selling everything from cashews to candy apples to Dickee-Dee triple-flavor cones.

"I've got money," I protested.

"Me too," Pro announced. "But I said it first, so treat's on me. What d'ya want?"

I settled for a Fudgesicle, which was ridiculously expensive, while Prometheus bought himself a red-white-and-blue popsicle that went by the name of Yankee Delight.

"You know what I don't get?" I said, when I was down to sucking on the popsicle stick. "I don't understand how you come to the planetarium for the first time and get a guided tour of the projector and the control panel, and I've been here five times and all that ever happens to me is that some guard tells me to move along before the next show starts."

"Maybe there's a couple things you gotta learn, Moonkid," Prometheus said, concentrating more on his Yankee Delight than on me.

"Like what?"

"Like maybe you shouldn't act so much like you is the greatest thing on God's green earth, 'cuz you ain't."

I protested. "I don't do that."

"Yes, you do," he said, not scolding so much as informing. He was passing on this information the way somebody might mention that you had a drip of ice cream on your chin. "Probably think it, too. Guys can see it on your face."

"My face?" I said, ignoring the rest.

"Yeah," he said, slurping down the last bit of his Yankee Delight. "That's the second thing. You gotta smile more."

"I smile," I said. "I smile a lot."

"No you don't, man. Most of the time, you look like your pet goldfish just died, you know? Kind of serious. People like to see people smile. It makes 'em smile when you do, y'understan'?"

"Well, I guess," I said, a little stunned. I wondered what expression I had on my face at that moment. It's hard to tell without a mirror, really.

Was I smiling? Did I ever smile?

"No big deal," Prometheus said. "But you ask't, so I told you. Sometimes I think it's kinda funny, you know? For a kid so smart, like you, there's a whole buncha stuff you never figured out. Maybe that's my job. You gotta teach me to read good, and I gotta teach you how to smile."

With that, Prometheus smiled broadly at me — and kept smiling — until I didn't have any choice but to grin right back.

Chapter 12

Journal, Sep 30

Moonkid and ~~me~~ I went to the Planetarium on Saturday. We had a great time. The show was about the sun and the ~~erth~~ earth and how they get along. It starts off with a bunch of slide ~~pro~~ projectors that put a city up on the dome. It's cool. Then the lights in the city go off — all because of sunspots.

    Ms. Noble, you should go to the show. It'll teach you a lot about how ~~improtent~~ important the sun is. If earth had a ~~orbet~~ orbit more further out, we'd all freeze. If we ~~was~~ were closer, we'd all burn. So earth is in just the right spot for us. I think it's cause that's where God wanted us to be, but Moonkid say it just ~~be~~ is an ~~acksid~~ accident.

The sun does other stuff to us too. Those sunspots can make power go crazy and change the ~~wether~~ weather and maybe even make the stock market go up and down. So if you knew what the sunspots ~~was~~ were going to do, you could make a lot of money. Then you wouldn't have to teach school ~~no~~ any more, Ms. Noble. You wouldn't have to teach ~~no~~ any more kids like me. Think about it.

You ~~probly~~ probably think our sun is pretty big, but it's not. It ~~be~~ is a lot bigger than earth, but as far as suns go, it's only medium size. There's suns in the Milky Way so big that our whole ~~soler olor~~ solar ~~sistme~~ system could fit inside. That'd make me boiling mad — get it?

I got have lots more to tell you about the planetarium and the ~~zye zeus~~ Zeiss star projector, but I'm gonna save it for my next journal. Bye for now.

Chapter 13

I should have known it wouldn't work. Schools don't work. Teachers are only quasi-competent. The whole school system is so corrupt and inept and otherwise floundering that it makes our federal government look good in comparison. Okay, so maybe it's not that bad, but you get the idea. Schools are dungeons of torture and incarceration where, should something honest, humane and exciting actually happen, the administration will quickly stomp on it before the whole enterprise is endangered by the wild enthusiasm of kids for learning. It would be too much for the system to bear.

I'm getting a bit cynical; forgive me. Cynicism is not a becoming quality for humans, much less for lost inhabitants of another planet. Let me get back to what happened on the Wednesday, so you can understand.

I walked into Fairfield Middle School, as usual, listening to the charming kindergarten kids shouting, "Kick his ass" out in the playground, sniffing the ripe odor of rotten milk and industrial-strength floor wax, staring up at Group of Seven reproductions yellowed by time and somewhat bedaubed with dried stains from now-unrecognizable food and drink. I was, quite literally, expecting nothing special when I knocked on the door of Ms. Noble's classroom and peered through the small window.

She came to the door, looked at me briefly and then averted her eyes. It was the first time Ms. Noble had ever looked away, instead of right at me; perhaps that should have clued me in. She smiled when she spoke. "Ian, I'm afraid you'll have to see Mr. Donaldson."

"Okay," I said, "I'll drop in after I finish with Pro." I was smiling, dumbly.

"No, Ian. You'll have to see him now." There was a falling tone to the now; and maybe that should have clued me in, too. But I kept smiling like the proverbial village idiot.

Off I went to the office, where only one secretary sat, chewing a gum which left both her lips and tongue slightly tinged with green. "I guess Mr. Donaldson wants to see me," I said, not waiting for her to look up.

"Who?" she said.

"Mr. Donaldson, your principal," I said, a bit snarky.

She frowned. "I mean, who are you? I've seen your face, but I can't be expected to remember the name of every Tom, Dick and Harry who walks in here, can I?"

Obviously not, I thought. "Ian McNaughton. That's M . . . C . . . N —"

"I can spell," she snapped.

I bounced on the balls of my feet while she buzzed through on the world's oldest intercom, announced my presence to someone at the other end, and told me to go ahead to the inner office. We did not exchange smiles as I passed.

Mr. Donaldson's office was done in vintage public-school-principal, a decorating style that is heavy on naugahyde, cheap veneers and bookshelves that don't match. Propped on one shelf was a picture that I took to be of his wife and daughter, both relatively attractive. I found this surprising since Mr. Donaldson himself bore a remarkable resemblance to a Bassett Hound. Perhaps in his youth, before the cheeks began to sag, he had resembled a young Tom Cruise. Time had not been kind.

"Sit down, Ian," Mr. Donaldson said. His gaze turned to a wooden slat-back chair that would have fitted right in a sleazy detective's office in a 1930's black-and-white film.

I did as he suggested. The chair was remarkably uncomfortable.

"Ian, I'm afraid we have a problem," he began. This is the kind of phrase principals always use when they mean to say, "Ian, you have a problem." I have never understood why they so generously join in on a problem that would inevitably be dumped back on me.

"What's that, sir?" I asked. I used my best, most humble, let's-get-to-it voice.

"Your tutoring of Pro, uh, Prometheus, is just not working out to everyone's satisfaction, I'm afraid."

This was the third time I'd heard "I'm afraid" in the last five minutes, but with no other evidence that fear was running rampant at Fairfield Middle School.

"How's that?" I asked. I was beginning to get it, as they say. A nagging doubt began to crawl around inside my stomach, like one of those creatures from Chekov's ear in *Star Trek 2*.

"There's been a complaint," Mr. Donaldson went on, "about the way your tutoring is . . . uh, well . . . undermining the regular class work."

"Undermining?" I said. The image seemed a bit much. I pictured Ms. Noble swinging a pickax, a coal-miner's helmet on her Afro, digging away just over my head.

"Undermining," Mr. Donaldson repeated. At least we were agreed on the word.

"So how have I been doing this undermining?" I asked. "And who complained? Pro wouldn't complain. Pro *likes* the way we go at things. His work is *improving*, sir." When I get upset, I begin to talk in italics, like that airhead Genevieve Boucher. It's most annoying.

"I'm afraid, Ian . . . " There was that phrase again. " . . . the decision has already been made. Ms. Noble and I spoke about the matter and there's really no choice." He looked up with those Bassett Hound eyes, full of sadness, you'd think. "I'm afraid your tutoring has to end."

"End?" I repeated stupidly. A sudden flash — Markdale Secondary. How would I ever explain this to Mrs. Greer?

"That doesn't mean your efforts here haven't been appreciated," Mr. Donaldson went on, managing a smile that somewhat lifted his cheeks, "because they have been. I understand you and Prometheus have hit it off reasonably well. But sometimes these things just don't work out."

"But *sir*, I protested, "they've been working out just fine. Pro's journals have *improved*. His reading is better than ever. We even took a trip together to the planetarium last week, for his journal."

"So I understand, Ian," he said dolefully. "But there has been a complaint and a decision had to be made. I'm certain your volunteer efforts would be appreciated elsewhere in the community —"

I cut him off. *"Elsewhere?"*

"Yes. There are seniors' homes and the mission down on Queen Street. I understand the food bank is always looking for help."

"So I'm fired?" I said, thinking: *kaput, canned, sacked, banished, exiled, reviled* . . .

"Well, you were never hired, Ian. You're a volunteer. Sometimes we no longer have need of particular volunteer services and that would be the case here."

For a Bassett Hound, this man spoke remarkable bureaucratese. I used to wonder if principals went to a special school to learn how to talk like that: smiling, cheerful, apparently sympathetic, glutinously polysyllabic. And all while they're verbally slapping you in the face.

"So I'm out?" I don't know why I kept sitting there, asking questions. The intent of all this was quite clear: *laid off, redundant, unnecessary, turfed out, rejected, despiséd* . . .

"That would be one way to phrase it," he said, forcing a smile that raised both his Bassett Hound cheeks and his too-small-to-be-a-dog's ears. When I didn't move, he decided to press the matter. "Now if you don't mind, I've got to get on with my other work."

I got up, stunned. What about Pro? What about Mrs. Greer? What about Markdale? This guy was sentencing me to death or dismemberment or worse.

"If you have any of Ms. Noble's books," he added when I reached the door, "perhaps you could return them."

Mr. Donaldson smiled. He obviously thought a missing copy of *Springboards for Reading Achievement* constituted a real loss to the whole educational establishment.

In the outer office, one secretary was engrossed in a copy of *Soap Opera Digest*, the other was typing a document with so many layers of self-copying paper it seemed as thick as the sandwich I had had for lunch. Neither of them looked up at me.

I left the office and began walking down the hall, mechanically. I suppose someone watching my progress would have noticed a certain robot-like quality to my movements. Then again, no one was watching. I fumbled in my backpack, looking for the copy of *Springboards for Reading Achievement* and finally lugged it out. At least my backpack would be lighter now, I told myself, attempting a smile. Why should I care? I could find some other kind of volunteer work, just like Donaldson said. I could serve soup at the mission. I could maybe be a literacy volunteer at the library. Mrs. Greer couldn't send me to Markdale without giving me a second chance, could she?

I'm good at telling myself things — always have been. I make excuses or reason things out or argue devil's advocate. I consider the broader picture or analyze using appropriate logical categories. I do all this until nothing means anything. But lately something new has begun to happen when various kinds of dung hit the rotating blades of my life. I've started to get this sense in my gut, or my bowels, or my stomach that something is terribly, terribly wrong. Not intellectually or theoretically or abstractly wrong, but wrong. In the gut. Where it hurts.

I reached the door to Ms. Noble's room, book in hand, and peered through the chickenwired glass at the class inside. Prometheus was sprawled in his desk, his body too big for the elementary school standard-issue furniture, his eyes on Ms. Noble who was writing something on the blackboard. *There's been a complaint*, I thought, and looked at him. His eyes were bright, happy. Maybe relieved.

I pulled back from the door and felt an enormous pain in my chest and then a smarting at the corners of my eyes. I couldn't understand what was happening at first. Could this be a coronary? At age sixteen, was I having a heart attack? But then it all came clear. From down in the gut I felt something twist my breathing and then there was this sound. A sob. And for a second I thought I was going to cry.

This would be an extraordinary thing for me. In fact, I can't remember the last time I cried: not when my mother left us, not when the cops threw my dad in jail, not when Billy Martin, the grade five bully, decided to use my nose as a punching bag. Crying wasn't something that beings from my planet did.

But here was this sob, and this feeling. Maybe if I'd let them come, there would have been tears.

But I didn't. I got myself back under control, as they say, stiffened my upper lip and all that. I walked out to the front steps of the school, and in the bright sunlight outside I felt better. The pain in my chest disappeared. The smarting at my eyes went away. There were no tears to wipe. All that remained was a sense of despair and a touch of anger. I couldn't do much about the despair — which seems an integral part of earthling life, if you ask me — but I was ready to take action on the anger.

I sat down on the steps and began ripping the pages out of *Springboards for Reading Achievement*. Then I balled them up and did foul shots into a wire garbage can, one page at a time, two points for each dunk. When the book was reduced to its cardboard covers, I had scored 640 points.

Chapter 14

Journal, October 5

*Ms. Noble I got to rite this journal myself today
cause Moonkid didnt show up. Maybe he got sick,
I dont know. Its not much fun to rite this with no
help from nobody and nobody to read it and bug
me to fix it. So i aint going to fix it up and dont
feel like writing much. I wisht Moonkid called to
say hes sick or whatever be wrong with him so I no
what happend. Unless maybe he got sick of me
and then I dont wantto know. I seen enough of
that. Ill do better next time.*

Chapter 15

I understand rejection. As far as I can figure out, rejection is natural among earthlings. Acceptance and community are the rare items. I imagine that this character trait will ultimately doom the planet. Currently, it's sufficient to keep away visitors from other solar systems. The superior beings of other planets, for whom love and support for each other are as ingrained as sex and aggression are in humans, probably look at earthlings with the kind of bizarre fascination an entomologist has for centipedes. Interesting creatures, but would you really want to have tea with one?

So the natural condition of man is to be rejected, isolated and lonely. That much is clear. I have understood this for ages, the truth having been pounded into my skull in school playgrounds and on corner lots years before my mother left us and went off to California. Not that I can blame her. Given the abysmal state of my father at the time, the general disarray of the family, the looming threat of the law and the constant interference of Granny McNaughton, any sensible person would have headed for the hills. It just would have been nice if she'd sent a postcard or two. For *that*, I blame her a lot.

Libby thinks I'm too hard on her. "Too judgmental" is her phrase. And I will admit my mother has done her best to make it up to us in the years since her escape: cash gifts, plane tickets, visits, stopovers, expensive Christmas presents, and the like. But I can't help how I feel. It was my mother who taught me about rejection and loneliness and despair; those wonderful lessons that aren't on the school curriculum. Those important but miserable lessons.

Anyhow, my state of mind when I returned to my house should be pretty clear from the chapter preceding. I did not have the energy to open a book or turn on the TV or unwrap a candy bar. I was so depressed that not even my F&I index would elevate. I merely sat in the living room listening to the clock tick, the refrigerator hum and the furnace fan rattle.

"So what's-a-matter you?" Libby said in her

best fake Italian accent when she breezed in the door. It's an annoying mannerism she picked up from one of the new boyfriends.

"Nothing," I replied.

"I didn't ask for the contents of your brain, Ian," she said, smiling idiotically. "I asked what your problem was."

"I don't have a problem."

"Just like you don't have a volcano-sized zit on your forehead."

I reached up and felt the skin. Unfortunately, my sister's descriptions are often deadly accurate.

"So what's the matter, kid?" she said, sitting down in the chair across from the couch. "Maybe your big sister can help."

I stared at her. This was a kind of *Leave it to Beaver* scene, where Wally helps his younger brother work out some trauma at school with thirty seconds of friendly advice. Except ours was more of a *Family Ties* family than a Beaver Cleaver household. And I've never found thirty seconds of advice useful for any problem more substantial than whether to put spaghetti or tortellini underneath the microwaved tomato sauce.

"Do you have to be so relentlessly cheerful?" I said, irritated by her grin.

"Why not?" Libby said. "I gave up industrial-strength depression for Lent. Besides, I got good news today — Mom's coming in for a visit next week."

"I feel honored."

The smile left my sister's face. At least I was successful in that. "Ian, anybody ever tell you that you've got an attitude problem? Anybody ever say that you make Roseanne Barr seem friendly and cheerful by comparison? You've got a chip on your shoulder the size of a —"

"A two-by-four," I suggested.

"More like a four-by-eight, a couple of 'em."

"I've heard such things said," I told her.

She shook her head, giving up. "Then there's no sense me trying to cheer you up. You're impossible, Ian. You're depressing and stubborn and stupid, like some mule or donkey always aimed in the wrong direction." She got up and began moving towards the kitchen.

"Thank you," I said, feeling my gloom rising up again. "I needed that."

"It's what you deserve, Ian. Now I've got to throw together a quick supper. Do you want spaghetti or tortellini with the sauce?"

I didn't answer. It seemed to me that the particular pasta made not a bit of difference; that nothing, in fact, made a bit of difference. I remained where I was, on the couch, staring straight ahead like a psychotic in a catatonic fit until Libby had supper ready and my father came in from work.

My dad hung up his old jacket on the coat rack, then pulled off his running shoes with a sigh of weariness. I used to describe my father as an aging hippie because of his fondness for dope, facial hair, vegetarian food and phrases like "chill out, man." But since reaching forty, Rick has mellowed somewhat. He still holds to his vegetarian diet and spends time every day in meditation, but no longer says "like, wow" to describe something that is simply "cool." He keeps his beard trimmed and his hair pulled back into a respectable ponytail, just the sort of look you'd expect from the owner of a middling-successful off-campus bookstore. Perhaps it is this change of appearance which stops the authorities from harassing him the way they used to, or perhaps my father has now become a collaborator with those he once regarded as the enemy.

"A bad day. A no-good, very bad day," my father muttered. He's lately started to quote children's stories at supper rather than bits of the Communist *Manifesto*. I worry that this could be the beginning of Alzheimer's.

"What happened to you?" Libby asked, serving up the tortellini.

"Customers crawling all over the place," Rick said, sitting down at the table. "University kids think I should have every book their professors mention in class. Professors think I should stock monographs on Venetian porcelain doorknobs, or get them in two days. Linda tells me she's quitting in two weeks to go to Nepal and seek inner wisdom. And I catch two little kids shoplifting. Lovely day."

"What were the kids trying to steal?" Libby asked. "Let me guess — Kant's *Critique of Pure Reason*?"

My father ignored the sarcasm. "Book tapes. Two of 'em. Should never have gotten those tapes in. If somebody wants to read a book, they should read it, not plug it into a tape deck. The kids probably thought Charles Dickens was some rap group."

"Isn't he?" Libby asked, grinning.

My father shook his head, a gesture which caused the tomato sauce already on his beard to look even more like a squashed red butterfly. "And what keeps you so cheerful today?" he asked her. "And what makes you such a downer?" he said, turning to me.

"I didn't even say anything," I told him, since it was the truth.

"You don't have to say anything," Libby piped up. "Your mood travels with you like a little cloud over your head."

"What's the matter, Ian?" my father asked. "That Ryan character hassling you at school again?"

I stared at the two of them. This was a real switch from the old days. Back then, my father would be off in cloud cuckooland and Libby would be the one to find a bandaid for my cut knee or a metaphorical bandaid for my bruised soul. But Libby's gotten out of the bandaid business lately so my father's had to become a bit more dutiful. I'm not sure it comes to him naturally.

"Look, nobody's hassling me, okay? I'm fine. I had a fine day. No problems. See, I'm smiling." I consciously ordered the risorius muscles at the corners of my mouth to contract, and there it was — a smile.

"That smile is about as genuine as Granny's teeth," Libby pointed out. "I can't imagine that the one person in this family who actually regards himself as an articulate, if not a brilliant, creature from another planet should find it so hard to talk about what happened to him today."

"This is one of your tutoring days, isn't it?" my father asked.

"Yeah," I said. "But I'm not doing that any more."

"What happened?" Libby asked. "What about your deal with Mrs. Greer? I thought you wanted to stay at Donlands rather than get your head kicked in at Markdale?" She took a breath. "I mean, Ian, have you checked your brain lately?"

"Libby, would you get off his case?" my father said to her.

"Just asking," she replied in that voice of pseudo-innocence.

I stared at the two of them. Why not let them have the truth, I decided. *Know ye the truth and the truth shall set you free*. Who said that? Anyway, it was worth a try.

"I was fired."

"Fired!" Libby said. "You can't be fired. You're a volunteer!"

For a second I saw my sister as she used to be, the scrapper for justice in the schoolyard, the outraged picketer of the American Embassy, the Liberty who actually lived up to her name.

I tried to explain. "That's what I said when the principal told me. So I suppose I was unvolunteered. You know, turn in your *Springboards for Reading Achievement* and clean out your desk. Except that they never gave me a desk."

"So what did you do?" Rick asked.

"I left," I said, feeling a bit embarrassed about it all.

"You just left?" Libby repeated. "You walked out of there without making a stink, or complaining to anybody or writing a letter to the Board of Education?" She looked at me as if I really were an alien.

"Well, I was thinking —"

"Did you at least talk to Prometheus and tell him what happened?" Libby kept on.

"I was going to, but he was in class so there wasn't a chance."

"The kid probably thinks you abandoned him," Libby said.

"There was a complaint," I explained.

"No way your student would complain," my father broke in.

"It's probably the teacher," Libby added. "She finds that you're actually teaching the kid a thing or two and she gets threatened. You can't give up just because of her. There's a principle at stake here, not to mention the kid himself."

My father and I both stared at Libby. It had been a long time since we'd seen her quick anger at social injustice. Maybe the old Libby was just buried deep inside this fashion-conscious, lipstick-toting, right-winging university identity she'd created. Maybe the old Libby was just waiting for something like this to bust out.

"So what can I do? I'm not allowed back inside the school," I said. "They've got the power. I'm just a high school kid." I looked at Libby. "A *short* high school kid, as you sometimes remind me."

"Your height has nothing to do with this," Libby replied. But I could see she was stuck for any more constructive ideas.

My father was quicker. "First of all," he said, "I think you've got to tell that Prometheus kid what happened. It certainly wasn't his fault. And then maybe you two could launch a protest at the district office —"

Libby cut him off. "Dad, this isn't the seventies," she said.

As the cliché goes, a silence fell. It's a funny image, if you stop to think about it, as if silence were some kind of *thing* waiting on the ceiling to tumble down when everyone starts thinking. But silence there was, while the gears ground in the three minds at the table.

Libby broke the quiet. "I think you've got to continue the tutoring. The kid's got motivation and he's making progress, isn't he?"

"Yeah, but how?"

"How about after school?" Libby suggested. "You use your spare period to do homework, and a couple times a week you meet Prometheus after school to do whatever it is you're doing. That way you're keeping your deal with Mrs. Greer, so long as you don't get in trouble in the cafeteria."

It's funny how a good idea really does set off gongs and turn on lights when it suddenly appears out of the gloom.

"That's perfect," my dad added, his eyes brightening. "You could do the tutoring here, or at the bookstore, or I'm sure the library would give you a room."

"Maybe you should ask Prometheus where he'd like to have the tutoring," Libby corrected.

"Yeah, right," I agreed. "But before that, I'd better find out if he actually *wants* the tutoring to go on, or if it's just me. Maybe he wants to call it quits."

"And miss out on the chance to spend a couple hours a week with the only resident alien on planet Earth?" Libby said. "The kid would have to be crazy."

* * *

The next day I sat on the steps closest to Ms. Noble's classroom, considering the nature of reinforced concrete. I read somewhere that Canada is a world leader in reinforced-concrete technology. This was offered as a kind of patriotic boast, the way someone else might say that the United States is a world leader in aerospace technology, or Britain a leader in medical technology. And I suppose leadership in something is better than leadership in nothing, even if it happens to be reinforced concrete.

The reinforced concrete steps leading from Fairfield Public School, however, were obviously produced before our world leadership was established. They were discolored, chipped, rounded, and flaking at some points to virtual rubble. I can point out, however, since I was looking at them closely, that they did provide housing for several thousand ants who were busy doing their ant-tasks with the silent concentration we expect of them.

Visitors from another planet, observing the humans across the street in their reinforced-concrete apartments and the ants beneath my buttocks in their reinforced-concrete home, might wonder why the ants were so busy and the humans so aimless. Just which species really is the intelligent life on earth?

When the bell went off at 3:30, I stood up on the concrete steps to avoid being trampled by an emerging horde of grade twos and threes. These kids burst out of the school as if fleeing an explosion, then suddenly slowed down when they reached the playground. There they sniffed the free air of the real world, and began tossing tennis balls or racing around or cheerfully smacking each other over the head with lunch boxes and book bags. If that kind of pent-up energy could ever be harnessed in the classroom, it would turn our coal-fired, industrial-age schools into veritable nuclear reactors of education.

The bigger kids emerged more slowly than the little ones. It should be pointed out that neither the boys nor the girls looked directly at each other, which says a great deal about the effective-ness of peripheral vision. Humans are such strange creatures. Just when they begin getting really interested in sex, they get too embarrassed to look at each other. Even dogs and cats make more sense.

Eventually the outpouring of kids slowed to a trickle and Prometheus came out the doors. He frowned into the bright outside light, then scanned the asphalt playground as if looking for someone. His focus was so far in the distance that he didn't see me standing at the foot of the stairs.

"Pro," I said, to get his attention.

He looked my way, surprised. There was still

no smile. "What you doing here, Moonkid? They said you wasn't coming no more."

"Who said?"

"Ms. Noble."

"Well, don't believe it. Mr. Donaldson fired me," I said.

"Ms. Noble just say the tutoring thing ain't working out. That's all. I figured maybe you got something better to do and just took off. Or maybe at the planetarium I did something wrong, you know."

"No, it wasn't like that," I said. "They just don't like me — Donaldson and Ms. Noble. They came up with some kind of complaint about me and said I couldn't come into the building any more. You complain to anybody?"

He gave me a look. "C'mon."

"Your mom complain? Anybody you know complain?"

"My mom don't even come near this hole on Parents' Night. How's she gonna complain?"

"Well, Donaldson said that somebody complained, so either he's lying to my face or Ms. Noble wants me gone. It could have been her."

Prometheus shrugged. He obviously had enough fondness for Ms. Noble that he didn't want to blame her, and I didn't know enough to make the case more forcefully. At the operative level, it didn't make that much difference.

"So what we gonna do now? If'n you can't come

into school, how you gonna tutor me?" Prometheus stared at me for a second, then caught sight of something over my shoulder. He shouted: "Amos, you stop that! Amos!"

I turned to look and saw a younger, smaller version of Prometheus kickboxing with another grade two kid. Both of them were smiling, so I suppose it was some kind of game, the way another generation would have played marbles or twirled hulahoops. But the way they were going at it, one of them would be crying pretty soon.

"Amos! What'd I say?" Prometheus yelled.

That stopped Amos cold. He looked over in our direction just long enough that the other kid could deliver a haymaker right to his side. Amos fell to the asphalt, sudden tears replacing the smile of a few seconds before.

Prometheus stormed over to them. "What you do that for?" he bellowed, either at Amos or the kid who hit him.

In the face of Promtheus' anger, Amos tried desperately to hold back his tears. The other kid cowered by the fence as if he expected Prometheus to pound out his halogens. I suppose I would have cowered too if two hundred pounds of angry black teenager began coming at me with the kind of expression Prometheus wore on his face just then.

"I didn' mean it. It was 'naccident," the kid stammered, ignoring the simple fact that a punch to the mid-section is never, ever delivered accidentally.

"We was just goofin' around," Amos agreed, his tears forgotten as he rose from the ground.

"You goof around too much," Prometheus told him. "You remember what I told you, what Mama told you. And you —" He turned to the other kid. "You wanna kickbox, you kickbox with me. You get one shot," he paused, "then I get one shot. Y'understand?"

"I didn' mean it," the kid repeated, not quite getting the gist of the message. He obviously thought that simple mercy was called for, while Prometheus was offering him a sporting proposition.

"Get outta here," Prometheus ordered, disgusted with the kid or his stupidity. "Amos, you come along."

Amos followed along meekly, looking at his brother the same way Prometheus and I looked at Ms. Noble. Sheer size commands a certain respect.

"You see what I gotta put up with?" Prometheus said to me. "I gotta make sure the kid gets home every day with nobody kickin' his head in. No wonder I got no friends around here." We walked across the street while a crossing guard held back approaching traffic. "So how we gonna do this tutoring thing with you kicked outta school and me lookin' after Amos?"

Very practical questions. Somehow responses

like, "We can go to the library," or, "Let's take the bus to my dad's bookstore," didn't make much sense. I was flummoxed.

"I thought, maybe, after school a couple times a week . . . " The sentence was left open-ended, like some kind of fill-in-the-blank quiz. Trouble was, I didn't have a good answer.

"Yeah, that's okay, but where?"

"The library?" I asked. It sounded pathetic, even as the words came out. Amos was up in front of us now, doing headstands and cartwheels. If ever a kid needed a tranquilizer to slow him down, Amos did. He'd have the local librarians pulling out their hair or calling Children's Aid, unless Amos had already unplugged their phones.

"Not so smart," Prometheus said, thoughtfully. "For somebody with all your brains, Moonkid —"

I finished for him. "I sure can be stupid. You have any better ideas?"

"Yeah, my place," Pro replied. "Ain't nothin' going on there except the TV blastin' away. You can handle that, can't you?"

"I guess."

"I'll just bring the stuff home from school, and you can help out. Oh, yeah, and I got this 'stronomy book I want you to look at it. It's cool."

"Sure," I said, amazed by how easily this had all been resolved. "Glad to."

"But I gotta check with my mom," Pro said. "You know how it is."

I nodded, a bit stupidly, because I really didn't know how it was. Even when my mom was still living with us, it was Rick we checked with.

"Let you know Wednesday, okay?" Prometheus closed. His eyes were up ahead on Amos and a group of kids lounging around some parked cars. The kids gave the general impression of having just relieved the vehicle of its stereo and hubcaps.

"Fine," I said, heading off to my bus stop as Prometheus went deeper into the housing project.

"Oh, Moonkid," Pro called, when I was a short distance away. "Thanks for comin' back. I 'preciate it."

Chapter 16

Journal, October 7

Ms. Noble theres one thing I don't get. How come you tell me that Moonkid ~~tutr~~ ~~tutring~~ being a tutor to me ~~aint~~ isnt a good thing and Moonkid tell me that you and Mr. Donaldson got him fired. Moonkid say there's this complant. So who complaned? Not me. I think Moonkid helpt my spelling alot and he got me to rite bigger ~~senteco~~ sentencs too. And thats not even counting the trip to the Plantarium.

So we got a plan, Moonkid and me. But I don't know if I can trust you enough to tell you about it. I thought you was on my side, kinda like a friend. But now I'm not so sure. Maybe you can talk to Mr. Donaldson and then Moonkid can come back here. It ~~wood~~ wouldnt be so bad. Think about it.

Chapter 17

I got the message through my father. Somebody had called the store, asked for Moonkid, then left a message that "tutoring at Pro's place is okay." So on Tuesday, I went down to the office to explain the change to Mrs. Greer.

"You're going to tutor where?" she said, lifting one blonde, fuzzy eyebrow.

"At the kid's house," I said.

"Because you couldn't get along at the school."

"No, I got along just fine. It's just that they didn't get along with me."

Mrs. Greer made a strange sound with her mouth, something halfway between a cluck and a slurp. She frowned, her two fuzzy eyebrows coming together over her fairly prominent nose.

"But I'm still tutoring," I blurted out.

"I'm doing what you said."

"Ian," she sighed, "the idea was that you should learn something about getting along with people."

Easier for me to master quantum physics, I thought to myself. "But I am, Mrs. Greer. I haven't been in trouble even once this past month. And I've built a good, solid relationship with Pro — the kid at Fairfield. Even ask Ms. Noble and she can tell you that his work is improving."

She looked at me. I shivered a bit, then gripped the side of my chair.

"And I really don't want to end up at Markdale." It sounded a little pathetic, but it was true.

"All right, Ian. Just stay out of trouble on your spare, that's all. Understand?"

"Yes'm," I said, in my most polite, abject and respectful voice.

I actually felt more comfortable sitting on the cold concrete steps of Fairfield Middle School waiting for Prometheus and Amos than going up, as I used to, to the school library. Unlike the library, which was painted institutional urine-yellow and smelled vaguely of dust and decaying paper, the outside world was glorious. The leaves were turning yellow and gold, the breeze blowing dry and warm, with dust that made the air itself seem golden. It was one of those perfect days that you see in movies, though they need smoke in front of the lens and a hundred klieg lights to get the same effect.

I just wished the sound track matched the image in front of me.

Two kids playing basketball. "Eff it, man. Eff that."

"I got two, you got nothin'."

"Yeah, yeah, yeah. Montreal sucks. You suck." A lay-up.

"What the hell? How you —" Another lay-up.

"Oh, sh—! SH—! SH—!"

Even with the offending letters removed, you can get the general gist of the conversation.

My father once told me that you could tell someone's social class by the way they filled in the thinking-time pauses in conversation. Somebody, someplace did a study. The working classes fill the holes in conversation with profanity. The middle classes favor "uh" and "like" and "well." The upper classes don't even bother filling the pause, they just leave the listener hanging in silence. If you're a member of the aristocracy, you naturally expect people to wait until you've constructed your next brilliant thought. Obviously these kids didn't think anybody would wait that long.

Amos appeared at the door before Prometheus. He came over to where I was sitting and began bouncing a wet tennis ball on the ground. I smiled and tried to look friendly, but the kid didn't pay much attention to me. We both just waited while the other kids rushed out of school. After five minutes, the rush declined to a trickle. After ten minutes, the trickle became a drop or two of kids who had been kept late. I started looking at my watch while Amos tried to figure out how high a soggy tennis ball can bounce. Finally Prometheus came out the door.

"Where were you, man?" Amos asked accusingly.

"Stupid Ms. Noble had to talk to me," Pro grumbled. "Last time I ever tell her something. C'mon, let's go. Amos, put that ball away."

Amos did as he was ordered and the two of us fell into step behind Prometheus who was barreling ahead like a runaway train. Obviously his interview with Ms. Noble had raised his personal F&I index to new levels. Obviously, too, he had no immediate intention of talking about it.

We crossed the playground and the street at full throttle, stopping two cars and a forty-ton streetcar in the process. We didn't slow down or say another word until we were halfway into the housing project, when Amos dallied to take a drink from a water fountain and Prometheus decided to wait up for him.

"How come you can't never trust nobody?" Pro asked.

"Wish I knew. People just aren't very trustworthy. That's how humans are, I guess."

"They oughtta be different," Pro said, looking back at the school. "What the people like on your planet?"

"I'm not really from another planet," I demurred, "I just like to pretend I am."

He gave me an impatient look. "I know that. But what kind of planet? What kind of people?"

"Trustworthy, kind, loving, dependable — all those things," I said.

"Lemme know if you find a spaceship going up. I wanna buy a ticket," he said, smiling for the first time. "Amos, let's move. Mama's gonna think you got your head kicked in again."

We walked a little more slowly through the rest of the park, winding our way between low-rise and high-rise buildings set between stunted trees and worn lawns. These buildings were part of a 1960's plan to tear down whole city blocks of junky Victorian housing and replace them with whole city blocks of junky concrete-block housing. The advantage was supposed to be green space where kids could play without the danger of being hit by cars. No one anticipated that the danger of street gangs or crack dealers would ultimately prove to be far more serious than colliding with the odd car bumper.

The green space was unusually empty right after school, a strange fact given the thousands of kids who lived in the apartments around it. The emptiness may have been due to the kinds of people we saw lounging on parked cars, or in stairwells, or propped on the concrete ledges of what were once fountains. The loungers had a vaguely dangerous look about them, as if you'd be likely to find a weapon beneath their toques or in the pockets of their Chicago Bulls jackets.

We passed one lounging group, and a face that I recognized stared over at me: it was Z or Z-Boy or whatever his name really was, the kid who had mouthed off to Prometheus on that first day in school. Now his eyes widened to take in the three of us, and then turned back towards his little gang. I didn't make much of it at the time. Maybe I should have.

Prometheus lived in a building at the far end of the park. A plaque proudly displayed its name, the William C. Diggs Building. I wondered who Mr. Diggs was to get his name on a building designed to warehouse the poor, and why he didn't merit something a little more upscale.

The building itself was five stories high, done up in red brick with dried-out concrete fountains installed near the entrance. It seemed pleasant enough, even welcoming in a way, except for the heavy grillwork over the first-floor windows and the loud rap music blaring from an open window on the fourth floor. The lobby was clean in an antiseptic, institutional way; the brown elevator doors recently painted.

We took the elevator up to the fourth floor and stepped off into a different world. The lighting was dim and fluorescent, the long corridor dingy and smelling strongly of disinfectant, the doors bolted with more locks than you'd find in a detention center. In this case, the locks weren't to keep the inhabitants in but to keep the outside world out.

Pro's apartment was 403, the first two numbers neatly nailed to the door, the 3 dangling upside down. Prometheus used two keys to unlock the door and stuck his head inside. "We're here," he announced, then waited for some kind of answer. None was forthcoming, but we could all hear the TV in the living room blaring some message about a detergent cleaning whiter than white.

"Ma — is it okay?"

A muffled "yeah" was the reply, so I followed Pro and Amos into the apartment.

Once inside, Pro flipped the two door locks back to their closed position. In the corner was an iron bar that provided additional security, apparently not needed in the middle of the afternoon.

The place itself was as neat and clean as any I'd ever seen; certainly a fair deal cleaner than my own house or the kitty-littered home of my grandmother. The decorating seemed to be Sears Colonial, with comfortable furniture in muted plaids with pine accents. The curtains were yellow-brown, to coordinate with the walls and carpeting. All in all, it might have been a photo from *Colonial Home* magazine, except that you had to go through a disinfectant-smelling hallway to get in.

I followed Prometheus to the living room, where his mother sat on the couch watching an enormous television set. I wondered how the TV had ever fit through the doors, or whether it'd had to be lifted by crane to the balcony and then brought in through the patio window there. It made our nineteen-inch set at home look like a toy, or a TV for leprechauns. I was so awed by this, and the enormous image of Oprah that appeared on it, that I hardly noticed Pro's mother until she spoke to me.

"Hello, Ian. I've heard about you."

"Nice to meet you, Ms. Gibbs," I said.

"Sisson, really," she corrected me. "I'm not a Gibbs any more. I'm glad you're gonna help Pro with his school work. He needs it. He's gonna be somebody some day, aren't you, Pro?"

"Yeah, sure," Pro agreed. He was paying more attention to the screen, where Oprah was going on about the topic of the day: husbands who got beaten up by their wives.

Mrs. Sisson was thin and small-boned, maybe five feet five, with large eyes, sagging cheeks and thick lips. At one time, I guess, she would have been pretty, but now she looked old. The only resemblance between the small woman on the couch and the hulking almost-teenager beside me was in the lips, a kind of expression they had in common.

"Mama, can I go outside an' play?" Amos asked.

He, too, was looking at the TV rather than his mother.

"When Pro's got his work done. You gonna work in your room, honey?" she asked him.

Pro nodded, and we left her and Amos sitting in front of the TV listening to the first abused husband, a burly truck driver.

"This room belongs to me and Amos," Pro said as he led me back. "We fixed it up a little."

On one side of the bedroom was a ghetto blaster, a bookcase with games on it, and a study desk with a bent-arm light. A poster of some angry-looking black guy and a taped brochure from the planetarium were on the same wall. On the other side was a set of Colonial-style bunk beds with teddy bears, plastic demons and several deformed Transformers on them. Two model airplanes hung down from the ceiling on black thread. Unlike my room, which has not been cleaned in living memory, and looks it, this room was as neat as a pin. The clothes were in the closet or the matching dressers, the games were stacked neatly on shelves, even the two wooden chairs looked as though they'd been polished with furniture wax.

"Ma cleaned it up a little," Prometheus said, probably in answer to the amazed look on my face. "You think this is gonna work okay?" he asked, moving towards a chair.

"Yeah, I think it'll be just fine," I said, though the room was less than ideal. The chairs and desk were fine, but the booming voices of Oprah and the abused truck driver were a bit distracting. I hoped the television noise would become like the "Om" of my father's meditations, something that you just didn't notice after a while.

"So what did Ms. Noble assign you today?" I asked.

"Got a new story to read," Pro said, pulling out that book I loved to hate, *Springboards for Reading Achievement*. "You got your book?"

I pictured the crumpled pages in the garbage bin outside Fairfield School. Best not to mention that, I decided. "I think I lost it," I lied, "someplace in the nuclear bomb site I call my bedroom."

"That's okay," Pro said. "We can use this one. The story's 'Lenin and the Ants' or something."

"'Leiningan versus the Ants,'" I corrected.

"Right. So I guess you know it already. She got up to 'bout here in class and say we got to finish it up at home." He stopped and looked at me. "It's a pretty good story. You think they really got ants like that?"

"I think they do," I said, "though I don't ever want to find out for sure. You get to the part where he has to make a run for the gasoline?"

"Not yet. We're here," he said, handing me the book. "Maybe you could read it? It goes faster like that."

"Maybe you could sit over here and follow the words when I read," I said. "It'll pay off, long term."

"No probs," he said, pulling his chair beside mine.

I put the book on the desk and began reading about Leiningan's problems with several billion quite hungry, quite intelligent ants — while a booming male voice from the living room told how his ex-wife had wrestled him to the ground and threatened to cut off various parts of his body. Prometheus seemed to have no difficulty at all concentrating on the story, perhaps because flesh-hungry ants really are more interesting than abusive wives. I was the one who became distracted. Maybe growing up, as I did, in a house without TV isn't all it's cracked up to be. Or maybe I have a deep-seated fear of angry women equipped with Swiss Army knives.

We finished the story in half an hour, then tackled the questions Ms. Noble had assigned. She certainly knew how to lay on the work, even if I had some reservations about the work itself. Prometheus' reward for all this would be getting to watch a 1940's black-and-white film based on the story the next day at school, but only after a test in the morning.

I quizzed him about some parts of the story, just to give him some practice, then wondered if we should try to write out a few answers in advance. But there wasn't time for that, or to help Pro with his journal. By five o'clock, Amos was at the door, begging to go out, and Pro's mother had to leave for her job on the hospital night shift. Pro was to be baby-sitter and security guard for the rest of the night.

I said goodbye to the three of them while Pro's mother talked about what was supposed to be served for dinner, and Amos begged for a chance to play baseball with a plastic bat so big that even I could hit with it. Pro ignored most of this, undid the two locks to the hallway, and said thanks as I headed off. I'd see him Thursday, same time, same place, same routine.

I walked down the hall to the elevators, pressed the button, and waited for what seemed like several eternities in the hallway. When neither elevator had shown up and I was ready to gag on the smell, I followed the red exit sign to the stairs at the end of the corridor. I went skipping down the first two levels with alacrity.

On the third floor, I met a group of kids coming up from the lobby. I had heard them on the stairs, the colorful f and s words bouncing off the concrete walls in a cacophony of profanity. It sounded a bit like sound bites dubbed and overlapped, the ultimate electronic rap.

The talk stopped when we met on the third floor landing. There were five of them, all junior high school kids of varying sizes and hues, all wearing the Chicago Bulls jackets and oversized toques that must have served as a kind of uniform. I recognized only one of them — Z-Boy. The others were a mixed crew of various sizes and races. What they shared was a disposition — surly.

"Look at this," Z-Boy said when he noticed me, then added a profanity or two for emphasis.

"What you doin' here?" asked the biggest of them. He was a very black, black boy, maybe eleven or twelve, but already bigger than I'll ever be. His tone of threat and braggadocio was obviously for the benefit of his group, who laughed on cue.

"Just visiting," I said, attempting to smile amiably. It was a handy phrase, from the days when Libby and I spent hours playing Monopoly, asking whether or not our man was in jail or just visiting.

"Just visiting," repeated a short but stocky white kid who looked like a junior Sylvester Stallone, probably without Sly's art collection or the mansion in Bel Air.

"You know, like Monopoly," I said, smiling as best I could. "Do not pass Go. Do not collect two hundred dollars."

This little witticism did not go over well.

"Funny guy," said the junior Sylvester Stallone.

"Real funny," said another.

The vaguely malevolent faces in front of me turned quite thoroughly angry at that point. Obviously humor was the wrong approach to this particular group. The five of them stood like a roadblock two steps below me. There was no way

I'd get by them if they didn't let me. I began considering a hasty retreat up the stairs. But to what? The welcoming locked doors of the fifth floor — if I made it that far.

Z-Boy spoke up. "He been hangin' out with Pro. I seen him at school and now —"

"You some kind of narc?" one of the others asked.

I didn't know if a strategic lie would be more effective than the dull truth. What happened to narcs in situations like this? Aren't they wired, with backup cops ready to storm in and get them out? I opted for the truth.

"Not a narc. I'm a tutor."

"Sounds like a narc to me," the biggest one said, coming up a step to the one below mine. We were pretty much face-to-face at that point. I thought about raising my hands to protect myself but decided not to. If you get attacked by a swarm of bees, they say, the stupidest thing to do is try to beat them off with your hands or outrun them. You're supposed to retreat slowly and carefully, accepting the odd sting without flinching.

Calm, I told myself, stay calm. There was this tingling up and down my back as the adrenalin surged in, the autonomic nervous system doing for me what it used to do for Neanderthals facing woolly mammoths. *Don't look afraid.* Easy to say, hard to do when you're scared to death. I tried to meet the big guy's gaze, but he wasn't really looking at my face. Maybe he was trying to locate the most lethal spot to hit me.

Z-Boy came up beside him and began poking at me with one finger. "Pro's a fool and his mother's a stuck-up cow, and you, you be —" There was a phrase I didn't quite get, but it made the others laugh.

"Listen, guys," I said, not sure what kind of reasonable argument I was going to put forward. Saliva had gotten stuck in my throat so it was getting increasingly difficult to talk. What was the line they always use in movies for situations like this? Ah, that's it: "Look, I don't want any troub —"

I wasn't able to finish the cliché because the smallest of them, a little Vietnamese kid, came up and plowed me in the gut. I felt the pain do a quick burn, and then had a clear sensation that I was about to throw up. Given our current positions and the likely trajectory of my vomit, the five of them would certainly come out the worse for all this. I was even thinking of warning them, trying to find some breath to actually speak, when I heard a voice from up above.

"What you doin'?" it said, deep and angry. With all the echoing and the pounding of feet it took me a while to recognize the owner of the voice: Prometheus.

"Z-Boy, Abdul, Rug, what you doin'?" He was just above me on the stairs now, and all their eyes were on him. "Moonkid, you okay? These guys buggin' you, man? I'll bust a couple heads."

"No, no, it's fine," I lied when I got the breath to speak. "No problem. We kind of, like, bumped into each other on the stairs."

Prometheus stared at me, unbelieving. I wasn't even sure why I didn't tell him the truth. Maybe I didn't want to make a big issue out of things, or figured that I could make peace with Z-Boy and the others by letting them off the hook. But I held onto the lie while I waited for the contents of my stomach to quit threatening a major explosion out of my mouth.

"We was just sayin' hello to your bud," Abdul, the big guy, explained, suddenly cowed by Pro's presence.

"That's right, Pro. No big deal," the junior Sylvester Stallone agreed.

The five of them split up, two heading into the third floor hallway, the others going farther upstairs, passing Amos as he came down with his plastic baseball bat.

"What happened?" Amos asked, all excited now. "They beat the crap outta Moonkid? What —" His words were cut off when Prometheus cuffed him on the head.

"Told you not to cuss," Pro said, as his brother's eyes filled with tears. "Nothin' happened. Nothin' gonna happen to any friend of mine."

I looked up at Prometheus, standing on the

step above me like the Colossus was said to have stood over the harbor at Rhodes. The idea of protection was a wonderful one, but actually accomplishing it might be rather difficult.

The three of us walked in relative silence down the stairs to the lobby and then out into the dying light of the afternoon. Amos was still smarting from the cuff to his head. Prometheus was frowning both at me and at Amos, as if we were both stupid kids who were likely to run out in the street and get hit by a truck unless some adult was looking after us. And I was still worried about throwing up, especially as my stomach contents were sloshing around like several socks in a washing machine.

Prometheus didn't have much more to say until we got near a makeshift baseball diamond and Amos ran off with the bat to home plate. Then Pro gave me a little advice. "Next time, take the elevator, Moonkid. It's a little slow, but a lot safer, if you know what I mean."

I knew exactly what he meant. I managed to smile and say goodbye with those words of advice ringing in my ears. And I almost made it to the bus stop before my stomach decided to reiterate Pro's wisdom. With half a dozen heaves, I managed to decorate a bush with the remains of both lunch and breakfast. Next time, I told myself, I'll definitely take the elevator.

Chapter 18

Journal, Oct 13

Ms. Noble you make me mad. You say we can rite what we want in this journal. Then you give me ~~oh trobl~~ a hard time when I rite what I think. That stinks, Ms. Noble. You shouldnt do that. Now I cant trust you no more.

You shouldnt fire Moonkid because he's my friend and he helping me do better. Even my mom says so. There ain't no complant against Moonkid except mebbe from you. But if I get a chance theres gonna be a complant from me. I'm gonna write a letter to the board of education. Just you wait.

I got lots more to say, but I aint gonna rite it for you. I'm ~~gonna~~ going to keep my own journal from now on. You cant read it Ms Noble even if you beg me. I'm going to keep my thots in my own head from now on.

* * *

My journal, #1

Hello, me. This journal is for me from me. Moonkid say it be a good thing to rite to yousself when you think about somethin. He calls it ~~flectv~~ re-flectiv writing. Theres a big word. Not bad, Pro. You can be pretty smart, sometimes.

Im not doing no more journals for Ms. Noble because you cant trust her. I dont know why. Ms. Noble is black like me so I thot I could trust her but I was wrong. She's a snake and a ~~b////~~ and a ~~////~~.

That feels good. My mama wont let me say those words but it don't mean I dont think em. I think alot of things I dont say so maybe Ill just rite a couple of them down. This is just for me anyhow. I won't even let Moonkid read it. I'm gonna write a letter to the bord of ~~edca~~ education about Ms. Noble, but I won't use those words. I'm just gonna tell them what she did, so then maybe they'll let Moonkid back in the school. It just aint fair what she did.

It make me think the world's a pretty lousy place. I don't like to say that because it don't help

Amos or my mama or nobody to think like that, but it is. Yestrday Abdul and Z-Boy and that gang amost beat up Moonkid. For no reason. Last week they beat on some kid in Amos' class cause he wouldnt give them a quarter. Can you believe that — beat up some little kid for a quarter? That's what I mean about this world. Moonkid, he like to think he come from some other planet, like Superman. But Moonkid's a little ~~weeerd~~ ~~wierd~~ *weird. What we got wrong is all right here, on earth. Stupid guys and crazy guys and angry guys. People that beat up little kids. People that mouth off to your mother. An old man that takes off just when you need him. It stinks.*

Sorry, me. That's how it is. I hate it.

Chapter 19

This week, I have been pondering the torture of physical education: payback-time for all of us gifted in the cortex rather than the biceps. As the jocks suffer through math or English, stumbling over simple algebra or rhyming couplets, so we intellectuals suffer through phys. ed., stumbling over sodden football fields, challenged by parallel bars, unable to deal with the complex problem of hitting a small ball with a large bat.

I have been trying to hang on to these thoughts the way a drowning man clings to a hunk of drift-wood, as I grit my teeth and hold my nose through gym class. My rescue won't come until the end of the semester when I will have finally completed the one compulsory gym course I have to take to graduate. (The rest of the phys. ed. requirement I can meet with a course in health education that promises videos of sexual organs damaged by various sexually transmitted diseases — oh joy!) Meanwhile, I tromp off to gym either first or second period, depending on the day, surrendering my clothing to a metal locker already decorated with markered initials and mouse turds, putting on an exercise outfit that manages to be both stylistically tacky and offensively smelly, and heading out to the freezing gym to await the rest of the torture.

The torture for the next few weeks is to be basketball. Having already described my facility in that other ball sport, the one with the bat, let me say only that my facility in basketball is at a somewhat lower level. At least a bat I can hold in my hands and swing, perhaps not accurately, but swing in some fashion; and the ball is small enough that I can grasp it. A basketball, however, is so large that only a human freak could actually grip the thing in one hand, and it has a surface texture that makes even holding it in two hands a real feat. The rules, of course, virtually require one-hand manipulation of this object — bouncing it, shooting it, tossing it to other players — as well as a number of other skills best assigned to monkeys or other primates.

As I once said to my now-departed friend R.T., I have difficulty taking seriously any sport that requires players to be well over six feet tall and asks them to spend much of their time dribbling.

The word sums up the whole game. *Dribble, noun. a trickle or drip; verb. to drool or slobber, as in, "Please allow me to dribble on your shoes, Mr. Donaldson."* Imagine a game where you must dribble or pass to move the ball, and if you dribble inadequately, it is called *palming*, as in, "That short kid palmed the ball, sir." How else, I might respond, can one bounce this thing?

Then there are the shots. The goal in basketball is to get this oversized, rubberized thing through an elevated hoop, a hoop so placed that sufficiently tall people merely jump up and *dunk* the ball inside, but anyone of normal height must find a way to shoot it in. (I might add, on a personal note, that those of us of less than normal height must shoot the ball with the force of a cannon to get anywhere near the basket.) The various shots have names: *lay-up, hook, jump shot, foul shot, underhand, overhand.* All of these involve a fair amount of coordination of the deltoids, triceps, quadriceps and latissimus dorsi muscles. Otherwise the ball will fail to reach the basket or will be intercepted by the other team or will do something else egregiously wrong because basketballs, I find, sometimes have minds of their own.

Our gym teacher, Mr. Newman, had previously done a brief review of these shots and decided today to take our playing skills forward another notch by teaching the man-to-man defense. It is called a man-to-man defense, rather than a politically-correct person-to-person defense, because such an activity between people of two different sexes would be prohibited by law.

Man-to-man defense seems to involve a continual harassment of one's opponent, a harassment that is supposed to increase when someone shouts "full-court press." It includes slapping at your opponent if he tries to shoot, interfering with his ability to receive or pass the ball, and a certain kind of intimidating physical pressure on his body at most other times.

"Use your butt," Herr Newman said, in that highly sophisticated language for which he is known and loved. "Put your butt right into the other guy. Contact. I want contact."

Willie, whose butt is of some considerable size, raised his hand. "Isn't that a foul, sir?"

"It's only a foul when he shoots. When he's not shooting, you can stick your elbows into him if you want."

Oh joy, I thought.

"It's aggressive," the teacher said in answer. "Basketball is an aggressive game. Magic Johnson didn't get where he is by being a nice guy, so let's get serious. Stand up. I want half of you on the red line, half of you on the green. Let's go."

After some shuffling, two-thirds of us were on the red, one-third on the green. A shouted order from Herr Newman led to a cry of *achtung* from someone in the class and we reordered ourselves, roughly fifty-fifty. Then we were paired off. Naturally I was paired with Ryan, whose dislike for someone smaller, weaker and less agile than himself has only grown since our ill-fated baseball game. After a brief attempt to shift his position in line, so as to be paired with someone else, Ryan groaned and stood across from me.

"Try not to be too pathetic," he said, sneering only a little.

I was trying to think up a comeback line, something about tragic pathos or pathetic fallacy or criminal pathology, perhaps a pun which someone of Ryan's low intelligence might understand, when Newman began bellowing. "Okay, turn and face me. The guy on the green line, use your hip and push the guy on the red line to the wall. Got it? Now."

Ryan began moving at me, using his hip as a kind of battering ram. I did what any sensible person would do — I ran.

"No, no, no!" Herr Newman shouted. "Don't run away from him, Ian, push back. You're pushing for position."

"Push back with what?" I said.

"Your ears," someone suggested, *sotto voce*, and the class convulsed. Now, I will admit my ears are somewhat oversized, but the joke wasn't all that good.

"Your body," said an exasperated Herr Newman. "When push comes to shove, you've got to push. *Capishe?*" He came over right beside the two of us. "Okay, now I want everybody on the red line to push the guy on the green line to the center of the gym. Ready? Go for it."

Under Fred's watchful eye, I moved towards Ryan, hip extended, teeth clenched. In a moment, it was hip against hip. I felt like a Ford Fiesta trying to push a Mack truck. Ryan stood, legs spread for balance, his two-hundred pounds as centered on the balls of his feet as if he'd been rooted in cement.

Fred had turned away. "Use your hips and your butt," he shouted.

I tried butting, but that didn't work; I tried hipping, but Ryan just stood there. Finally, I gave him a shove with both hands. And that worked.

"Hey," he shouted, "that's a foul!" But I had him off balance now, and began pushing him across the gym floor with my left hip. The sight was so amazing that several other pairs stopped their pushing and shoving just to watch.

Herr Newman blew a whistle and we all stopped. I was red in the face from exertion. Ryan was red in the face from embarrassment. Josh and Willie were both laughing.

"I'll get you for this, you little —" was the thanks I got for doing my part of the exercise.

"Okay, scrimmage. You green line guys are shirts. Red line, pinnies." He took a little time to toss out the stained purple pinafores which would mark our team. "Okay, let's go. *Mach schnell*. Man-to-man defense, full-court press. I want to see aggressive. A . . . G . . . R . . . E . . . double S . . . V . . . E," he spelled out, omitting only a couple of fairly-important letters. "Use your hips and your butt. Stay with your current partner." Then he blew the whistle and threw out the ball.

I had barely got my pinnie on when Ryan started pressing against me, not to get in position for a pass, but to butt me right into a wall. I tried to get my balance back, but whenever I got my feet planted, he came at me from another direction.

"Move, move," the teacher shouted. "Follow the ball. Stay with your man."

The ball had somehow made it down to the far end of the gym, where Josh Brown went for an easy lay-up. Two points for their side.

"Okay, pinnies. Fight for position. Move that ball."

We all began running in the other direction: part of the herd-like aspect of basketball that I find so distressing. But the running kept Ryan off my back, or hip, as it were.

My team reached our basket and the ball, amazingly, made it that far as well. Somebody tossed the ball to Trevor, who panicked and threw it to Josh, but Joe Coniglio swiped the ball back, dribbled twice and went up for a shot. He missed, but Derrick Stevens got the ball and began looking around for somebody to pass it to.

I ran over towards Derrick, as if he might actually pass it to me, with Ryan right at my side. When I stopped, we started pushing and shoving hips so hard that I couldn't pay any attention to the ball or the game. It was just a matter of survival: fight back or get bowled over. So I have no idea how the ball ended up bouncing right at me. I wasn't following the play or the basket or the ball, I was worried about Ryan's aggressive butt. But there was the ball, in my hands.

"Shoot it! Shoot it!" somebody yelled.

Ryan stopped pushing at me and began jumping up and down to block my shot. He was already half a head taller than me. Add to that his jumping and the amazing anti-ballistic assault of his hands and I couldn't even see the basket, much less aim at it.

That's when a miracle happened. It was one of those moments that come to people only once or twice in a lifetime: like St. Paul on the road to Damascus or Charlemagne with his dream of battle victory over the Gauls. I heard this voice, this otherworldly voice say, *dribble past him and do a lay-up.* I heard it with a clarity that was nothing less than astonishing. *Dribble past him and do a lay-up.* It was a mystical moment, the kind of epiphany you read about in new-age self-help manuals. I felt a strange power surge up within me, a radiance, a mystic sense of oneness with the basketball, the game, the whole universe.

I bounced the ball, once, twice, and began

moving forward, bounce, bounce. And somehow I got under Ryan's arm and past him when he was jumping up. Now the way to the basket was clear, so I took the ball in two hands. *Do a lay-up*, said the voice. In dreamlike motion, I went up on one leg, the ball in one hand, the basket just ahead of me —

Then somebody grabbed my back leg.

I went spinning, losing my aim, the ball and my mystical moment all at once. The next thing I felt was a thud as someone's knee hit my head, and then I was chin-down on the floor while everyone else raced to the other basket.

After the shouting and screaming when Ryan dunked the ball, Herr Newman blew his whistle. He came over to me only to find blood streaming from my nose, creating its own kind of red line on the floor.

"Better get a towel, son, and clean that up," he said, with his usual compassion. "It's only a little blood."

* * *

"What happened to your nose, man?" Prometheus asked me when he came out of school. "Looks all swolled up."

"That's only because it is all swolled up," I said, because *swolled* is so much more expressive than *swollen*, suggesting both the appearance and the painful feel of my nose.

"So what happened?"

"I fell down playing basketball."

"It hurt?"

"Mostly my pride."

"That's the worst," Pro said, scanning the playground for his brother. "You fall flat on your face, that's bad, but a buncha guys see you fall flat on your face, that's the pits. Guess you play basketball like you play baseball?"

"That would be charitable. I'm probably worse at basketball. Because of my height."

"Height don't mean that much unless you wanna play NBA," Prometheus said, waving at Amos to come over. "It's speed and the moves, man. Maybe I can show you a couple things after you tutor me."

"It won't help. I'm spastic. I —"

He cut me off. "Moonkid, anybody ever tell you you got an attitude problem?"

I didn't reply. Several thousand people had suggested that to me, usually in a spirit of animosity. Prometheus was the first person ever to say so with even a smidgen of caring.

Pro paused to think. "Listen, man, if you can help me read better and write better, how come I can't help you play basketball better? Answer me that."

I couldn't. His logic was impeccable.

My lesson to Prometheus came first. He had gone to the library and checked out a couple of books on astronomy for a book report and was having trouble starting either of them. Some of that was understandable. He handed me Stephen Hawking's *A Brief History of Time* and said he couldn't get past page one. What could I say but that most of my father's university-educated friends have never gotten past page one? The difference is that they pretended to have read it, or to understand the ideas without reading it, while Prometheus admitted that he was stumped. We needed something a bit simpler.

Look to the Night Sky was a better book for us, shorter sentences, easier vocabulary, with a picture or two to help out the reading. "Go out of doors on a clear, moonless night . . . " it began, readable for Prometheus with hardly a stumble. As he went on reading, I was able to forget about my aching nose and embarrassment in gym. I went off into the night sky, circling Polaris in my mind, touching Ursa Minor, flirting with Cassiopeia, speeding the light years to Draco and Andromeda. It was a comforting universe up there, full of ancient stories and even more ancient stars, far away from this troubled blue-green planet with its blaring television sets and school-time humiliations.

"So how you like that?" Prometheus asked when he had finished Chapter Two. "You think I did good?"

"I think you did great," I said honestly. This was the truth. He'd needed my help only for the

Greek names and a few words like *constellation*.

"I'm startin' to read better thanks to you teaching me, Moonkid."

"Nah, it's just confidence and practice," I told him. "We've only been doing this for a little over a month. That's not long enough for me to have taught you much of anything. But I guess it helps to have somebody there when you get stuck on a word."

"Like Cass-peea. I'd never get a word like Cass-peea."

"Yeah, Cassiopeia's a tough one, all right. I imagine they called her Cassie for short."

"I'm gonna read some of this to Amos tonight. He's pretty stupid, but maybe this'll help him. Maybe I can show him some of these stars here in the picture. What you think?"

"The pictures are better than you can see in the city," I explained. "You really have to get out to the country to see much."

"So maybe we can take a trip some night to look at the stars," Pro said, looking at me. "Give me something to put in my journal."

"Sure," I said. "I'll see what we can do."

Prometheus put the book down and stood up. "Okay, now it's time for me to teach you. You ready?"

"Basketball?" I said. "It's late, Pro," I demurred, looking at my watch. "And it won't do any good. It's not worth the trouble."

"Listen, I thought we had a deal. The court's lit up, so it don't matter if it's gonna get dark soon. And maybe it'll help you a little. What you say to me, I just gotta have confidence and practice? Maybe that's all you need."

I suppose I could have said something about my real needs: greater height, better small muscle control, some coordination, a sense of timing. I could have gone on at length about my physical limitations, the genetic spasticity passed on from either my mother or my father or whatever alien culture actually produced me, my difficulties working with any group of people (and that included a team) on any project. But I didn't. The expression on Pro's face was clear: he wanted to teach me some basketball and he'd be hurt if I didn't let him.

So five minutes later we were down on an asphalt basketball court in the middle of the public housing project. There was no net on the basket, and the asphalt was quite uneven, but the carbon-arc lighting was truly impressive and made up for the declining light of the sun. The brightness also made me feel a little more secure, given my experience with the locals in the stairwell of Pro's apartment. Security = visibility^2 ÷ (m+M), where m equals the mass of the possible victim, and M equals the muscles he has to defend himself with.

"Okay, let's see you run and stop over there," Pro began.

"I know how to run," I said, insulted.

"I know you know how to run, but I wanna see you. I'm gonna throw the ball to you when you stop and turn, okay?"

"Okay." The kid was sounding like a gym teacher.

I took off on both my flat feet, thudding over to the edge of the court, then flipped around to face Prometheus. Except that my body was still moving, so I ended up going backwards as he bounce-passed the ball to me. The momentum and the force of the ball sent me sprawling into a pile of fallen leaves.

"I caught it," I said, to cover the embarrassment.

"Yeah, you did do that," Pro agreed. "You ever hear of a pivot?"

"Of course I've heard of a pivot," I answered back. I knew of pivots, pivot points, pivotal times in history. I could decline the word: *I pivot, you pivot, he pivots, we pivot, they pivot.* I could spell the past tense: *pivotted*, or is it *pivoted*?

"So why don't you do it? Stop on your left foot and swing the right one 'round. Got it? We'll try again."

I got up, went to my starting position and began running back. This time I stopped on my left foot and swung my right foot around so that I was at least facing the ball when it came at me. I caught it, but my hands stung.

"Do you have to throw it so hard?"

"That wasn't hard," Pro announced. "Maybe in a couple weeks, I'll show you *hard*. Right now, we gotta work on your feet. Basketball you play on the balls of your feet. You know, balls?"

I smiled. The joke was obvious.

"You gotta be dancing like this, all the time," Pro said, and began bouncing around on his enormous feet like some rapper gone wild. "Now you try."

"I'll look ridiculous."

"You already look ridiculous, man. I'm trying to get you to play ball. So you gotta dance on the balls of your feet, for balance. You try."

So I tried. I hadn't realized how leaden my feet actually were until I tried to bounce around on them. It required all sorts of leg muscles that I'd never used before. Not to mention this whole business of running, pivoting and throwing the ball. In twenty minutes I was exhausted, and I hadn't even taken a shot.

"When do we get to the lay-up?" I asked him.

"When you move so good you don't fall down. You gotta practice, Moonkid. Do a little exercise, maybe. Get the legs going. You got a basketball?"

"No."

"Okay, so I'll let you borrow this one. You gotta work on passing and dribbling. You know how to dribble?"

"Kind of."

"Let's see."

Dribbling is not an easy thing, unless it's from

the mouth, and it gets that much harder when somebody's watching you. Pro passed me the ball, I bounced it about three times and then lost the thing and had to go chasing after it. Now I may be bad at basketball, but I'm not that bad.

"Let me try again," I said after retrieving the ball.

"Use your fingertips," Pro told me.

"For what?"

"For dribbling," Pro said, slapping his head to show just how stupid I was acting. "You gotta get your palm outta there and just use your fingertips."

"Like this?" I asked, contorting my hand so it looked like a flesh-colored garden hoe.

"Yeah, but not so stiff. That's better. Now try to move with the ball. Bend over a little — gives you better control."

I stopped. Admittedly, I was doing a little better, but there was still a question in my mind. "Pro, who taught you all this?"

He looked like I'd just walked up and slapped him. The expression on his face was so strange that I was really sorry I'd asked. "A guy," he muttered. "Guy I used to know."

"Must have been a good basketball player," I said.

"Yeah," Pro said, "used to be." Then he grabbed the ball from my hands, went dribbling all around the court, deke-ing left and right, and went up for an effortless two-point lay-up.

We practiced for the rest of the half hour, despite my occasional protest and the gradually increasing aches in my legs, arms and wrists. I made no perceivable progress, though Pro kept indicating otherwise. In truth, I suspect my ball handling went from simply dribbling to a full-fledged drool as I got increasingly tired.

"Okay, Moonkid, that's enough," Pro declared when, in fact, it was far more than enough to exhaust this ill-conditioned alien. "I got something I got to tell you."

"Like what?" I said. "Like I can't play basketball? Like this is hopeless?"

"No way, man. Ain't nothin' hopeless. You keep practicin', you gonna get better. Simple as that. But listen up, I got to tell you about Joe."

"Joe? Joe who?"

Prometheus wasn't looking at me any more. "Joe, that guy I told you about, my friend. Had some trouble with Zed and those guys, same guys you met up with in the hall. Remember?"

"Oh, yeah," I said, a mental lightbulb flickering on.

"Well, there ain't no Joe. That's what I got to tell you." The harsh light over our heads gave a kind of sheen to Pro's skin. He didn't look at me. "What I got to say is . . . Joe is . . . me." He stopped and took a breath. "And that mom I told you about, that's my mom."

"Oh," I said. I was going to say something like,

157

I already knew that, but for once I was smart enough to shut up.

Pro took a quick look at my face, then turned away again. "So I just wanted you to know, 'cuz friends shouldn't make stuff up like that, you know?"

"Yeah, right. So how about that letter we worked on? Did it work?"

Pro smiled. "It was ace, man. The cops laid off us and put the heat on Zed and Ng and those guys. Maybe you noticed they ain't so friendly."

"I got that impression," I said, a remembered pain returning to my stomach.

"So that's it," he said. "You practice dribbling this week. I'm gonna work on my reading. Maybe we'll both be a little better next time 'round."

"Deal," I said, walking off towards the bus stop. But my mind wasn't really on that very reasonable trade-off we had worked out. My mind had been snagged by a single word that Prometheus had used — a word I hadn't heard since R.T. left, and not much before that in my life. Friends. I liked the sound of it.

Chapter 20

My Journal #2. October 24

Moonkid says it'll help me ~~rite~~ write better if he helps me write this journal. So I ~~aske~~ asked him, how come this journal ~~sposed~~ supposed to be ~~personel~~ personal if you get to read it. He says he'll only read it ~~ifn~~ if it ~~aint~~ isn't about him. So I said okay.

I'm helping Moonkid play basketball better. No ~~ofens~~ offense, but Moonkid ~~is a real spaz~~ is pretty uncoordinated. He can't run, he can't dribble and he can't shoot. So I got him going with running and dribbling. I kind of wonder how a kid can grow up so spaz, but Moonkid says he never played no sports. I guess you ~~gotta~~ got to learn to be coordinated like you got to learn to read and write.

My dad taught me how to play all kinds of sports. When I was little, I used to play ~~sock~~ soccer and baseball and basketball and ~~rest~~ wrestling, too. Like my dad. Funny, I don't think much about all that. There used to be some good times.

I'm still mad at Ms. Noble. She sent me a note about Moonkid, like she's real sad and this ~~ain t~~ isn't her problem. But who kicked him out? It was her. Thats what I hate about grownups, they say one thing and do ~~somehting~~ something else. I ~~say~~ said, if you so sad about Moonkid, then you let him tutor me in school like before. But she said no. She said I cant ~~ford~~ afford to miss the class time. B.S. is what I say, but I couldn't say that out loud. I just ~~thot~~ thought it.

Too bad you couldn't see me spell uncoordinated, Ms. Noble. See, I can use a dictionary now. I know how.

Chapter 21

I was dribbling the basketball out back of the house when Libby came walking out the door. I had actually started getting pretty good at this particular manoeuvre, bouncing the ball up and down at various heights, moving forward and back, even pivoting without losing it. It wasn't all that hard and didn't require the kind of physical dexterity or concentration I'd always imagined. It was really just a matter of fingertips and wrist action, and a certain dogged repetition. Since I was supposed to practice looking up when dribbling, I found I could even read the latest *Omni* while bouncing the ball with my better hand. This was exactly how Libby found me.

"Let me guess," she said. "You're going out for Hallowe'en as a very short Michael Jordan studying for his college degree, right? Or, no, the great brain has finally cracked and you're reduced to bouncing a ball up and down, looking at a magazine to remember the days when you could read, is that it?"

"I love your cynicism," I said, looking over at her without missing a single bounce. Libby was dressed in what is now her basic university outfit: expensive designer jeans, an appropriate sweatshirt with a pricy ski lodge logo in one corner, a pair of flat-heeled but obviously expensive shoes, and a smile that required more layers of lipstick than the layers of paint Ford puts on cars. "Look at this," I added, and began moving back and forth, dribbling high and low, finishing with a quick pivot that left me with the ball in two hands, ready to shoot.

"Should I be impressed?" Libby asked. "Have you decided to sacrifice the M.D. or Ph.D. for an N.B.A.? Ian, those basketball guys are tall. You, my brother, are —"

"Not," I concluded for her, tossing the ball at her with more velocity than was strictly required.

"Ooh," she said, deflecting the ball as if it were covered in slime.

"Afraid I might break one of those chartreuse-colored fingernails, Lib?"

"No, well, yes, but that's irrelevant." Every so often Libby has been known to use a polysyllabic word or two. She tries to resist this for reasons of social acceptance, but the vocabulary is in her genes, I think, and occasionally spills out of her mouth in spite of herself.

"So what's relevant?"

"We're going out to dinner tonight with Mom," Libby said.

Klunge. Noun. The rush of adrenalin to the heart when one realizes that an appointment has been totally, unforgivably and embarrassingly forgotten. Had I been dribbling, I would have lost the ball. Since I was now merely standing, my mouth dropped open. I was in danger of that other kind of dribbling.

"You forgot, didn't you," she said.

"Sort of."

"Not sort of. You forgot."

"I told Prometheus I'd meet him for practice after supper," I said.

"Practice?" Libby said, flashing me a peculiar look. The heavy lipstick gives her mouth an odd, deformed O shape in certain expressions. "Since when do you practice anything besides lessons in *Thirty Days to an Obnoxious Vocabulary*? Ian, Mom has flown in from California to have dinner with us. We have things to discuss."

This got my back up. "Correction," I said. "Our mother has flown in from California because she could get a stopover from New York at no extra cost. Our mother deigns to have dinner with us because she has no one more important to meet with tonight. And we, Libby, do not have things to discuss. *You* and *she* may, but we do not."

"A bit testy, Ian," Libby observed. "I seem to have hit a nerve. Perhaps guilt. Perhaps jealousy. Perhaps, well, who knows. Now, are you going to put on some decent clothes and join us for dinner or are you going to go off to some housing project and bounce a basketball? Which one will it be?"

I didn't have to think for very long. My mother made these periodic appearances in our lives, coinciding with plane trips and the usual statutory holidays, and then treated us to an obligatory dinner or highbrow cultural event. She apparently thinks these somehow make up for her sudden departure, seven years ago, and the dull, day-to-day parenting she does not provide — the bandaids, subway tokens, and pop bottle returns that make up the real life of families. Obviously I disagree. Nonetheless, there are certain ties, certain tugs, that keep me going through the motions of a relationship. I dutifully report for the dinners, join her for concerts, run out to the airport to say hello, and have even flown to California for one less-than-impressive holiday.

However, my ongoing life is not in California, but here, and not with her, but with a yuppying ex-hippie father and an oversized grade-seven kid named after a do-gooder Greek god. Prometheus and I had agreed to get together, to work on my ball-handling skills and to start the next lesson.

Somehow that felt important and dinner with my mother did not. And there was no question, if my mother were double-booked into dinner with us and dinner with a client, just who would be dropped.

"Say hi to her for me," I said. "I'll catch her next time."

Libby shook her head. "Suit yourself. We're going to Fenice if you change your mind. That is, if you still do have a mind." And off she went to let me stew in the juices of my own guilt.

I'm not really sure, admittedly, why those guilt juices should be mine. It was not *me* who disappeared, anxious to find my true self. It was not *me* who didn't even send a postcard or make a phone call for over a year. But whenever my mother shows up, I'm the one who seems to feel guilty.

Must be the human in me. Any self-respecting alien would be more rational.

When I walked over to Pro's place, I tried to keep my mind focused on basketball, thereby blotting out my mother. Basketball is wonderfully simple, in a way, and human relationships are not. Human relationships are full of loss and guilt and hurt and love, I suppose, and probably a few gazillion other qualities. They're messy and complex and troublesome. Dribbling the basketball on the asphalt court next to the William C. Diggs building was wonderfully simple in comparison.

Unfortunately, my skill level had fallen several

notches from my practice at home, either because I was distracted by other thoughts or because the asphalt was so uneven. Also, people were watching. A couple of old guys were talking and following my dribbling out of the corners of their eyes. A group of little kids were playing tag out on the lawn and sometimes took a moment to wonder who this short guy was and why he was bouncing a basketball so far from his home turf.

And that swell gang that had roughed me up in the stairway were lounging or lurking or loitering (depending on your point of view — theirs, mine, the law's) near Pro's building. I kept dribbling, losing the ball, chasing it, starting again, and ended up feeling hopelessly incompetent in the process.

"Not bad, Moonkid," Pro called from the other side of the fence. "I been watchin' you."

"From where?"

"From the window. Had to get the dishes done 'fore I could come down."

"I was better at my place."

"Yeah," Pro said, "and you'll be worse when you play a real game. Put a little pressure on, and you'll probably fall apart. That's why you gotta practice, lots, so you don't got to think about the ball. Y'understand?"

"Yeah, right," I said, grudgingly. "Did you see this?" I started doing my manoeuvre, moving towards the basket as fast as I could, dribbling high up to start, then low down as I got closer, finally turning in a pivot, and bounce-passing to Pro.

"That's real good," he said, grabbing the ball in that effortless way I had yet to master. "Now let's see you do that and go for a shot. You're real short, but you're kinda quick, you know, so maybe you use the quick to make up for the short."

He bounced the ball back to me and the pressure was on. Pro was watching, the two old guys were watching, a bunch of little kids were watching. If you counted the windows in the sur-rounding buildings, there might have been several thousand people watching me dribble to the basket and try for the lay-up. Of course I missed.

"Couple things," Pro began. "You gotta go up on the other foot. You're a lefty, so your left knee goes up and you push off with your right foot, get it?"

"My knee?"

"Yeah, for balance. And 'case anybody gets in your way. B-ball's a *mean* game, if you know what I mean. What's that big word? Aggress . . . aggres-sive. And there's the other thing. What you look at when you shoot?"

"The basket," I said. "What else?"

"Well, you're looking at the wrong thing, man. Look at the backboard. There's a couple sweet spots up there that'll make the ball bounce right in. You try to go swish into the basket, you're gonna blow a lotta shots 'cuz the angle and speed gotta be just right. Off the backboard, the angle's better and speed don't matter so much, so you got a better chance of sinking it. See?"

Angles? Speed? Velocity? Probability of shot success? This kid was talking geometry at a pretty sophisticated level. Maybe I had underestimated this game.

"Just watch," he said, grabbing the ball from me. "This is one sweet spot." He went racing up to the board, jumped up in the air, then bounced the ball against the backboard slightly above and to the left of the basket. In. Two points.

"Here's another," he said. "You gotta aim higher when the ball's goin' slower."

Once again, the ball bounced in for two points. "If you put a spin on the ball, you hit the board over left." This time he went up, aimed the ball, but the ball hit the rim, spun around and out.

"You missed," I said. Maybe I was relieved that he didn't sink them *all* the time.

"Yeah, I ain't so good with my left hand."

I groaned. Not only was Pro ten times better than me, he was ten times better with his *other* hand.

"Now you try," Pro said, tossing me the ball.

So I did, without much success. We spent half an hour talking about angles, spots on the backboard, speed of the shot, bounce rotation — it was enough to make my brain spin. Who ever thought mindless basketball could be such a complicated game?

"Moonkid," Pro said, as I went up for the two-hundredth time, "I don't think you got your brain on this tonight."

"Huh?" I said. My level of articulation declines when I begin sweating and my pulse rate goes up.

"I mean, you don't shoot *this* bad. You ain't even concentratin'. You gotta concentrate on the shot or it ain't never gonna work, but you're only half here, you know?"

"But I'm here," I protested. "I wanted to be here."

"I ain't talking about your body," Pro told me, shaking his head, "I'm talking 'bout your brain. Your brain off on some other planet. What'sa matter?"

"It's not . . . I mean . . . " Like I say, my articulation was not of the highest order. "I'm supposed to be having dinner with my mother."

"Thought you ain't got a mother," Pro said, taking a quick foul shot. Swish — two points.

"Well, I've got one," I said, "but she lives in California, so she's pretty useless as a mother. Except she's flown into town today and I was supposed to have dinner with her, you know."

"How often you see her?" Pro asked.

"Couple times a year," I said, then corrected, "Well, maybe not that often."

"So your mom flies in here to have dinner with you, and you come out here to play ball instead?"

"Well, there's my sister . . . she really wanted

to talk to Libby," I said.

"Moonkid," Pro started, staring at me open-mouthed, "you got something wrong with your head. We can play ball any time, but your mama's only here for, what, a day or two?" He waited a second, letting the situation sink into my brain. "You get your butt outta here and go see her. Then you practice a bit on your own and we'll get together when you got your whole brain on basketball. Now get."

He threw the ball at me with such force it almost knocked me over, then turned to walk back to his apartment. Lesson over — or lesson begun, depending on how you looked at it.

I turned, bounced the ball twice, took a shot and missed again. I looked at my watch: seven-thirty. If I went right away, I could make it to Fenice by eight.

* * *

"Would you like to check your ball, sir?" was how the maitre d' greeted me at the door. He kept a smile on his face, as if many other diners at Fenice appeared at the door in jeans and sweatshirts, carrying a basketball under one arm.

"Indeed, yes," I said, affecting a British accent. When entering a restaurant where every man is wearing a suit, I seem to automatically fall into that kind of nose-in-the-air tone.

I handed over the basketball and he gave me a claim ticket, propping the ball up in a coat closet with an assortment of men's hats.

"Come with me, please," he said, after I told him who I was there to meet, swishing his way into the restaurant, dodging tables and waiters as I trudged along behind, avoiding the quizzical looks of the other diners. Apparently my outfit was not *de rigeur* among the clientele of this establishment. Or perhaps it was the lingering odor of sweat and basketball that they could detect as I walked past.

Libby and my mother were at a corner table, engaged in an animated conversation. You can always tell when Libby is animated because a flush comes over her otherwise pale cheeks and she begins poking at the air with one finger, as if there were some invisible elevator button right in front of her and she was in a hurry to get to the next floor.

My mother seemed a little more relaxed. She was leaning back in her chair, perhaps to avoid Libby's finger, and smiling in a way that Libby calls benign and I call self-satisfied. She was dressed like most of the other female patrons at Fenice, in a stylish dress in some shade of puce, this season's in color, accented with garish gold jewelry and a scarf. She has taken to scarves, lately, as age accentuates the wrinkles on her neck, and forty-five years of gravity on her chin line takes its toll. Next year, I suspect, some plastic surgeon will be five thousand dollars richer and my mother's neck will once again be wrinkle-free.

It was Libby who saw me first. Her response was immediate: "Oh my God!"

"No, it's just me," I assured her as the maitre d' pulled out a chair for me.

"Ian," my mother said, remembering my name, "I'm so glad you decided to come."

I smiled. Otherwise I'd have to explain that my real motivation had more to do with Prometheus than with her.

"I'm not," Libby said, more honestly. "Ian, how can you walk into a restaurant like this, dressed like . . . that?"

I smiled at her. I wouldn't say that my dirty jeans, black sweatshirt with the number 42 in large letters (the ultimate answer to the ultimate question of life, the universe, and Douglas Adams' psyche) and red Converse basketball shoes fit in very well with the other male patrons, but I've never been very concerned about fitting in. "What's your problem, Lib? I checked my basketball at the door."

"You look fine, Ian," my mother said, pretending to be less bothered by my appearance. "But you might want to wash before dinner."

"And use some deodorant," Libby mumbled.

I smiled again, sweetly enough, and went off to the men's room to wash my hands, which actually were quite dirty, and my face, which is always fairly sweaty anyway.

The men's room gave me a chance to run water into a sink the shape of a clam shell, use a bar of soap carefully carved to resemble a seahorse, dry myself on a puce-colored paper towel made available for the purpose, and then to douse myself in the house cologne, Fenice Puce, or whatever, so I smelled like an habitué of a Spanish bordello.

When I returned to the table, Libby and my mother were once again engaged in conversation, this time a bit less animated. I sat down, picked up my menu, and began looking over a set of appetizers that each cost three to five times as much as a McDonald's McMeal Deal. A main course would likely be the price of a small used car. My mother, I assumed, was claiming us as a business expense.

"So, Ian, I guess you've heard your sister's big news," my mother said.

"News?" I asked, looking at Libby.

"About school. Transferring out to San José State," my mother went on, as if this should make something go click in my cortex.

"What?" I said. "Where?" I was reduced to monosyllables.

"I haven't told him yet," my sister intervened. "I was going to tell him the other day, but he was busy rushing out the door to this tutoring thing of his."

"Tell me what? What is this?"

"Libby is coming out to California to live with me," my mother declared, her self-satisfied smile becoming even more selfish and satisfied. "She's applied for transfer to San José State next semester, and with her marks there should be no problem getting in."

I kept staring at Libby. How long had she been sitting on this little bombshell? How long before she intended to tell me or my father? How long before she ran away, like my mother had, like everybody does?

"Earth to Ian," Libby said, probably trying to deflect my stare. "It's no big deal. I'll be around until January, anyhow."

"No big deal," I repeated. I saw her packing her bag — no, it was my mother — no, Libby packing up, suitcase after suitcase — and then the house, empty, just me, just us — and the vacant, doped stare of my father. Twenty images in the blink of an eye, one tug at my heart, one rumble in my gut.

"You might want to come out for the summer, Ian. Then we could all be together," my mother suggested. She reached out to touch my hand and several pounds of gold jewelry clanked in the process.

"No, no thanks," I said. Polite to the end. Granny McNaughton had told me to always be polite, even in the middle of it all, when my mom disappeared and my dad was in the detention center. "*Smile and be polite*," Granny would say, *"you are a McNaughton."*

The waiter appeared over my shoulder, dressed in black with a starched white shirt. There was some kind of talk. I couldn't concentrate on the words.

"What do you want to order, Ian?" my mother asked.

"Order?"

"Food, Ian," my sister said. "This is a restaurant. Customarily, people eat in a restaurant. What do you want to order?"

I stared at her, then at my mother, then back at Libby. There was this awful sick, sinking feeling in my stomach, like I'd been punched, like I was going to puke on the table. No, I couldn't do that. It wouldn't be polite.

"Sorry," I said, "I'm not feeling hungry. I . . . I don't feel that well, really."

"Ian, are you all right?" my mother's grip tightened about my wrist. Where had she gone, then, seven years ago, leaving us behind? Where was she now?

"I'm fine," I lied, politely, and then the truth came back. "No, not really. I mean, I'm sick. I don't want anything."

"Ian, you are being very weird," my sister announced gravely. "It's not as if —"

I cut her off by standing up. "Sorry," I said, "I can't stay for dinner after all. I've got to — I've got an appointment. I've got to —" Got to what? I couldn't think of any got-tos except "I've got to get out of here." My stomach was rumbling. My whole soul was rumbling.

"Ian, wait —" my mother called.

But it was too late. I was already moving towards the door, walking like a zombie in *Night of the Living Dead*, desperate for air, or the outdoors, or something. I passed by the maitre d' who seemed quite confused by the expression on my face.

"Sir. Sir —" he called after me. "Your ball, sir."

Chapter 22

My Journal #3. October 27

Moonkid is playing basketball alot better now thanks to I ~~showd~~ showed him a couple things. Maybe he ~~aint~~ isnt all that spastik after all. But he's still kinda strange. He didn't seen his mom for a whole year, but he comes to play ball with me instead of eating supper with her. Pretty dumb. Sometimes I think smart kids are ~~all screwed up~~ weird in the head.

Course, I ~~aint~~ haven't seen my dad in maybe five years, so what right do I got to talk. I gotta remember. Yeah, it was four years ago Christmas that the cops told him to keep away from here or they'd arrest him. That was after the court order, for hitting Mama and Tina. I hated him back then.

I wanted to hit him and punch him just like he used to do to Mama and Tina when he got drunk. Maybe Tina even deserved it, for the drugs and all, but he was wrong to hit her so hard. Nobody should hit nobody that hard. And Mama didn't do ~~nothing~~ *anything. She just tried to keep him from hitting Tina, and then she got it. That was the worst.*

I don't like to remember back then, because I was too little to do ~~nothing~~ *anything except cry and what good does that do? I was like Amos, but not* ~~no~~ *any more. My old man wouldn't try nothing now. Next year I'll be big as him. Then I'll show him. Maybe in the ring, Prometheus vs. Mount Olympus, match of the* ~~centry~~ *century. Come watch a kid punch out his old man. That would fill up the Gardens, all right.*

That's enough. I don't like thinking about this stuff. Moonkid gave me a new book to read, so I'm ~~gonna~~ *going to start it.* The Outsiders *they call it. Same lady which wrote* Rumblefish *so maybe it'll be good.*

Chapter 23

Hallowe'en has never been a particularly propitious time in our household. My father was busted one Hallowe'en; another year, his store got trashed. So Hallowe'en, for me, means a fair amount of personal embarrassment, if not fear, if not loathing.

On this particular Hallowe'en, to avoid further store trashing, my sister and I were to join Rick at the bookstore for a kind of literary trick-or-treat. Any costumed urchins who approached would be given a cheap piece of candy and a ninety-nine-cent Robert Munsch book.

"It's promotion," my father explained, pointing out that the ninety-nine-cent book cost him only sixty cents, and after tax considerations, maybe forty cents, which isn't any more expensive than a candy bar. Also, the ghost or goblin on the receiving end would have something to read while it was feeding its face with the goodies extorted from other stores and homeowners, thereby filling brain and stomach simultaneously.

"It's protection," Libby said, reminding us all of the Hallowe'en when my father's store was soaped, broken into, ransacked, vandalized and otherwise made the scene of some adorable adolescent hijinks.

"It's preposterous," I said, feeling silly in a black academic gown and a rubber mask that seemed to represent a ghoul with quite egregious skin problems: green and purplish blobs that made even my sometimes-volcanic pimples look benign. I was a ghoul that needed acne treatment.

"Ian, do you always have to be so depressed? You take the fun out of everything," Libby replied, rolling on some hideous purple lipstick. She'd been quite buoyant since meeting with my mother, nor did my father seem particularly upset that Libby was abandoning us. The only person moping around our house lately was me.

"I enjoy being depressed," I told her, which must have been at least partly true because I'd spent the last few days quite totally immersed in it. "Depression gives me an edge, a style, an existential reason for being," I went on.

"It gives me a headache," she replied.

When the first shrill "Trick or treat!" sounded

from down the street, Rick sent us to our positions. Libby was inside, by the cash register, with a basket of candies. Next to her was Linda, the part-time sales clerk who had not yet left to find her real self in Nepal, and was designated to pass out the little books. Overseeing them, and handling possible sales, was my father. And outside — in the cold, in the damp — was yours truly.

My role was relatively simple. I was to stand in a somewhat hunchbacked position — oops, make that spine-challenged — and wave children in while intoning "Book . . . candy," in a voice several registers below my usual squeaky tenor.

Why is it that ghouls are always afflicted with limited vocabularies? Why can't a ghoul say something like, *"We are cheerfully giving away books and sweets this evening, children,"* the way a kindly librarian might? But there are conventions in these things, standard forms and procedures. So I hunched over against the wind, cursed the ineffective long underwear, swung my right arm as if it were broken, and delivered my message, *"Book . . . candy,"* in such a terrifying voice that any sensitive little kid should have been frightened. Among the youngest group, some of them actually were.

Hallowe'en follows a progression very similar to life. It begins, cheerfully enough, with very small children dressed as Barney or a spider or a princess or in some garb they cannot yet identify.

They shout "Trick or treat" with no knowledge of its meaning, as a magic phrase which produces candies, goodies and attention. They enter houses and stores, receive stale candy or shrunken chocolate bars, emerge with glowing eyes and offer the occasional thanks (when prompted) before returning to the protective arms of their parents.

I enjoyed these kids, the six o'clock crowd, with their awe and wonder and terror. They were adorable, as perhaps I was at that age (despite oversized ears), full of enthusiasm for a school they can't yet attend, for parents who seem to have nothing better to do than cuddle and care for them.

I dimly remember those days myself, and the lopsided, floppy dragon costume my mother made for me. I roamed the streets of Mt. Forest secure in the knowledge that, only a few feet away, Dad stood watching. And behind him, waiting for us, was a home for Libby and me. A place where Mom actually made chocolate chip cookies occasionally, and Dad had lots of time to play or dance or sing with us because he didn't want to surrender much time to work. And we were happy. I remember being happy.

At six-thirty came the older crowd, the kids who had been in school long enough to discover what kind of reward they got for their previous awe, delight and wonder. These are the kids who had come to the sad realization that life was not about fun and games, but about various kinds of loss and heartache. Naturally, the outfits of these middle school kids were hipper, more artful, more contrived. "I'm Barney after a car accident." "I'm a Freddy Kreuger victim." "I'm a successful corporate lawyer — see my briefcase?" The eyes still had a spark, but the language was more demanding. "These are little kid books." "How come we don't get a *Mad Magazine*?" "Pretty cheap candy."

I was the same at age eight — smart before my time; knowledgeable with no knowledge. I dressed that year as a biker after a motorcycle accident, wearing my dad's old black leather jacket and my recently-departed mother's red lipstick to appropriate effect. I carried two bags for candy, deciding to be more efficient than previous years, but managed to get beaten up and have one stolen from me, because, for the first time, my father hadn't come along to ride shotgun. If Libby hadn't started pounding out the gang of candy-snatchers, I probably would have lost both bags. Libby was always there, someplace in the background.

It was in the six-thirty group that I recognized a face. Amos. I don't think he knew who I was, since that would have required either X-ray vision or some hint from Prometheus, who stood waiting at the curb.

"*Candy . . . book . . . for you, Amos,*" I said.

"Who you?" he asked, peering up at my rather disgusting face.

"You, Amos. Me, ghoul," I said, a neat twist on the old Tarzan and Jane line.

"How come you know me?" he said. His pirate outfit consisted of little more than a bandanna, an eye patch and a plastic sword, but he must have figured that disguised him completely.

"Ghoul smart . . . know much. Book in store, Amos."

By now Prometheus was cracking up, partly at my face and partly at the frustrated expression on his brother's.

"You's no ghoul. You's a people," Amos said, two debatable assertions. "Who you really?"

"I'm Ian," I said, lifting the rubber mask off my face. I hadn't realized how the mask trapped heat and moisture inside until I flipped if off. Suddenly the cold night wind froze my face.

Amos smiled. "Oh, yeah. You," he said, relieved.

"There really is a book inside," I explained. "My father is giving them away, and candy too."

"Your dad mus' be plenty rich," Amos said as he headed off through the door.

Rich is all relative, I thought of shouting after him, but decided against it. Even with the bookstore doing reasonably well, we still drove around in the oldest Volkswagen van in the city, lived in a house for which we paid Granny McNaughton only a nominal rent, and had a TV barely a tenth the size of that hulking monster in Amos' living room. If you want to see rich, Amos, you've got to see how my mother lives. How Libby is going to live. But I didn't say that either. Instead I put my mask back on to keep my face warm.

"Good outfit," Pro said, after I had my eyes lined up with the holes in the mask.

"Guy's got a complexion problem," I said, smiling even after it occurred to me that he couldn't see me do it. "What are you doing down here?" The words sounded aggressive, but I was really just curious. The bookstore had to be four or five miles from Pro's apartment.

"Came to scoop up some decent candy," Pro explained. "Down in the park, you only get junk. Got enough junk this afternoon, so we took the bus up here where you yuppies got some good stuff to throw 'way. Last house we hit gave me buncha change 'cuz they was outta candy. Probably got fifty cents for shoutin' 'Trick or treat.' Not bad, huh?"

"Not bad. And we're giving away these little books."

"I'm gonna get one too," Pro said.

"You've got to have a costume," I told him.

"I got a costume, man." He gave me that big grin of his. "I'm dressed up like a poor white kid from the slums, see?" he said, pointing to a theatrically-whitened face and a rattier version of the clothes he usually wore. "Not like the cool black dude I be most of the time."

Off he went into the store, and out he came with Amos and a book just a few seconds later. The poor white kid line must have worked with Libby too.

"Kinda wondered what your dad looked like," Pro said.

"Yeah?" I said. "What do you think?"

He thought it over. "Think you gotta take after your mom, Moonkid." Then he turned to look down the street. "You keep your eyes open. I hear some of the other guys from the park is comin' up here, and they ain't as nice as me and Amos." He noticed Amos was gone, then spotted him halfway up the block. "Amos, you wait up for me." He turned back. "See you tomorrow, right? Me teachin' you, right?"

He was off before I could answer. Since the basketball thing began, Pro was teaching me two days a week and I was teaching him two days a week, an arrangement he considered quite fair. Both of us were making slow progress. His reading was probably up to the level of the average grade six kid, which isn't that bad for someone in grade seven. And my basketball was at the level of the average high school kid encumbered by poor coordination, lousy reflexes, weak muscles and oversized feet, which isn't bad for me.

After seven o'clock, the little kids began to disappear and the night was taken over by gangs of teens and tweeners. The teens weren't bad, usually on the way to a party somewhere, or showing off their costumes, or out to scoff up a little candy to eat on their spare at school the next day. But the tweens, those awful kids in grade seven and eight, pumped up on pre-adolescent juices without the appropriate fear, guilt and embarrassing body hair that go with puberty, full of self-importance because real high school hasn't knocked it out of them yet, too young to be arrested and too old to be cuffed on the head: these kids are dangerous. And mouthy. "Nice head, man." "You ever hear of Clearasil?" And pushy. By seven-thirty, I think I'd been shoved, poked or prodded half a dozen times. At least two kids had pulled at my mask. And one kid had started ripping at my academic gown, as if the jeans, T-shirt and longjohns underneath might somehow be more interesting.

If I'd dressed as a medieval knight and carried a mace, quite a few tweener heads might have been seriously dented that night. As it was, I kept up my ghoulish act until eight o'clock when I was freezing. Two hours of this Hallowe'en foolishness was enough for anyone, even a ghoul with a lousy complexion, and so I went inside.

I was right behind half a dozen tweeners who were dressed in rag-tag costumes and dime-store masks. The kids were pushing and shoving, as expected, swearing a bit more than usual. They seemed quite intent on getting not only their book and candy but anything else that wasn't glued in place.

"You get one book," Linda was saying. Her voice had lost its usual spacey quality and now just seemed exhausted.

"One for my little brother," the kid said. His face was covered by a Freddy Kreuger mask, and he had two of the little books in his hand. The rest of his small gang were looking on.

"Tell your brother to come see us," Libby joined in. She was dressed in her degenerate princess costume, the one that makes her look like a cross between Morticia Addams and Cinderella. "One book, buddy."

"I ain't your bud," the kid mouthed off.

"Who you s'posed to be?" said another of the gang. "Some kind of ho?"

The others laughed. Libby was obviously considering slugging the kid. And I began to think about getting in a second punch.

"Okay, okay, we seem to have a little problem here," my father said. He was dressed like a New Age wizard, and sounded like one too.

"We don't got a problem. Just this thing here got a problem," said the first kid.

That was it. You can insult my sister once, but not twice. She reached out and grabbed the kid by his coat collar.

"Don't you —" Libby spat into his mask.

But my father intervened. "Libby, let's not —"

And then the kid was free. He pulled back from

Libby, muttered a quick, "Eff you," grabbed a handful of books from the basket in Linda's hands and took off out the door.

The rest of the gang followed suit, but not before stuffing half a dozen full-sized books into their goody sacks. The last one to leave, the biggest, swore at Libby one more time.

Which is when I lost it. I ripped off my stupid ghoul mask and tore out the door after them. The group had split in two, so I raced after the slower half: the kid in the Freddie Kreuger mask, a short kid in a pumpkin outfit, and a kid dressed, appropriately, as a prison inmate. We must have looked pretty bizarre to people passing by. I mean, how often do you see a guy in academic robes chasing three kids in masks, even on Hallowe'en?

The kids turned onto one of the quieter residential streets. I kept close behind them, slowly closing the distance between us. Halfway down that block, I started feeling quite winded. By the end of the block, I was ready to call it quits from sheer exhaustion. But I didn't get the chance.

The kids slowed up, then stopped running altogether. In a second, I had "caught" them. Or they had caught me. What now?

"Gimme the books," I said, gasping for breath.

"What books, man?" said Pumpkin Man, playing innocent.

"What you talkin' about?" asked the prison inmate.

"I'll give you somethin'," snarled Freddy Kreuger. And he did — a kick in my right side. If I'd been faster, or ready for it, or less winded, maybe I could have jerked out of the way. As it was, it got me right in the ribs.

"You little —"

I didn't finish. He kicked me again and I went down.

Then I was in trouble. On my back, I wasn't much of a threat to any of them, so instead of one kickboxer I had to deal with three kids who wanted to do me damage. I was down in a pile of leaves when one of them — I don't know which — kicked my right side again. This time I groaned, the pain welling up like a burn. Then I saw a foot coming at my face, but I managed to reach up, grab it, and push the owner away. Maybe he fell. I was too busy to notice.

The other two were at me, fast and hard, fists and feet. I tried to fight back, but couldn't find anything to hit. I tried to roll over onto my side and get up, but one of them jumped on me, and a barrage of blows to my face kept me on the ground. I ended up curled like a fetus, my hands over my head to keep it from being kicked, the rest of my body a punching — or kicking — bag for three little kids. The burning pain in my side was growing, a fire without any light.

Then the kicks died out. The next sound was something besides my own moaning, and fists hitting my flesh.

"Oh, man," cried out one of the gang, in pain.

"Don't! Don't!" cried out another.

"Outta here. Get outta here —" came the first voice.

I rolled onto my back and tried to see what was going on in the blur above me. I couldn't make much out in the darkness, but there was definitely a new shape up there. Somebody on my side.

"Libby," I grunted.

"You okay?" she asked, slightly out of breath.

"Yeah," I said, rolling on my side to get up. Then I corrected, "No."

I sat up and my head felt dizzy. For a second, I thought I might lose everything and pass out into the pile of leaves. But then the focus came back and the little white specks disappeared. I was back on Euclid Street, not far from my father's store, and Libby was standing over me holding on to a little kid in a Freddy Kreuger mask.

"Can you get up?" Libby asked. "If I have to help you, I'll lose this little jerk."

"Yeah, yeah. I can, sort of." I got up slowly, my side still aching, my feet looking an awfully long way away.

"You don't look too steady," Libby said.

"It's okay," I told her. "Where'd the others go?"

"They took off. I could only hold on to this one."

Libby held Freddy Kreuger in her grip. The boy behind the mask, the one who had been kickboxing so effectively was cowering now and groaning from some damage that Libby had inflicted on him. With the odds two-to-one against him, he was begging for mercy. "I didn't do nothin' . . . It was them . . . You can't do this . . . I'm gonna call the cops . . . "

Actually, we were the ones who intended to call the cops. Libby kept a firm hold on the kid's jacket. I got one of his arms behind his back into an arm lock, and we did an awkward three-person waltz back to the bookstore.

The lights were all on in the store when we arrived, but the book/candy giveaway was finished for the night. My father looked more than a little agitated when we came in the door.

"We only got one," Libby announced. I suppose that was obvious, but that's what she said.

"Are you two all right?" my father asked. "I mean, I couldn't see where you went and —"

Linda came in as my father dissolved into inarticulation. "We called the cops, but they say they're so busy —"

"Then I guess we'll just wait for them," Libby declared. "Let's see who this sucker really is."

She reached out, ripped the plastic clasp on the back of the Freddy Kreuger mask and unveiled our thief, my assailant.

I recognized the kid. He'd been one of the gang on the stairway. "I know you," I said. "They call you the Rug, right?"

He just stared at me, strangely mute. The look in his eyes suggested that he'd have spat in my face if he thought he could get away with it.

"You know this kid?" Libby asked. She, Linda and my father had a similar expression on their faces — amazement, disgust, curiosity, all mixed together.

"Yeah, kind of," I said. "He's a friend of — well, he lives near Pro. His name is Rug or Ruggiero or something like that."

"Oh, great," Libby said. "So what do we do now?"

The four of us were silent. I suppose it might have ended differently if the kid had struggled, or begged for mercy, or said anything to keep up the tension. But he was stone silent. It was late. We were all tired and wanted to close up.

"I think we should let him go," I said.

"What?" Libby cried, amazed. "I chase the kid two blocks, pull him off you, drag him back here, and you want to just let him off?"

My father was on my side. "I think Ian just wants to call it quits. The kid has lost all his candies anyway, and the books are long gone."

"I can't believe this," Libby said in disgust.

"It could be hours before the cops get here," Rick went on, "and he's a juvenile. Nothing's going to happen. You didn t get badly hurt, did you, Ian?"

"I'm okay," I lied.

My father turned to the kid. "And you won't

do it again, will you?"

I was half expecting the Rug to start mouthing off, but he just shook his head. "No, sir," he mumbled. The kid who had been stomping on my side with what felt like jackboots was now just a little sixth-grader hauled into the office.

"You two are crazy," Libby said. "Linda, what do you think?"

"Your dad's the boss," Linda replied, ever the good employee.

"So it's decided then," Rick chimed in, turning back to the kid. "We've got your name, Ruggiero, and we know where you live — so if there's any more trouble, we won't have any choice but to talk to the police. Understand?"

The kid nodded. He was smiling now. He was off, a free man, and he knew it.

"So don't get into any more trouble tonight," my dad lectured as he unlocked the front door to the store.

Rug was outside like a shot, not leaving time for anyone to have second thoughts on all this. The four of us stood in the now-quiet store, feeling suddenly foolish.

It was Libby who broke the silence. She stared at me, and then at my father. "I can't keep doing this, you know," she said. "I just can't."

I noticed there was blood on the knuckles of her right hand, not fake blood, the real thing. And I was beginning to understand.

Chapter 24

My Journal #4. October 31

Did pretty ~~good~~ well tonight. Amos and ~~me~~ I went out to the west end, out by the univercity. Those guys got so much money they can throw it away, or at least give it to every kid who shouts trick or treat at them. Amos got two bags of candy. That should keep him good and sick all week. I got a couple good things too, but the money was better. Amos and I picked up $5.68 in change, besides all the candy. Sure beats taking bottles back to the store.

Moonkid's dad ~~gots~~ has got a bookstore up there. First time I ever saw him and Moonkid's sister. She looks pretty good, specially when you think how funny Moonkid looks. Moonkid's dad seems like a pretty good guy. He ~~be giving~~ gave away all these little books to everybody ~~that~~ who came in. Wish I could give away stuff like that.

Funny thing on the way home. Saw a poster up with my old man on it. Mount Olympus in some ~~kinda~~ kind of big comeback match. Almost said something to Amos about it, but figured I better wait. I dont know what to do about it anyhow. ~~Werent~~ Wasn't like he called up and invited us to the ring or something. Guess I got to think about it some.

Besides that, Amos and ~~me~~ I had a real good time. No trouble, this year. Maybe Z-Boy and his gang ~~gonna~~ are going to clean up ~~there~~ their act. Maybe the moon is made of cheese, too. Anyway, looks like good stuff is coming down the pipe.

Chapter 25

"I think I would've killed the guy," is what Prometheus said the next day. He went for a lay-up with a kind of ballet-dancer grace that made no sense for a stocky kid with size-thirteen running shoes. Then he passed the ball to me.

"Well, we couldn't. He's a juvenile." I dribbled twice, went up with the ball despite the pain that still lingered in my side, and scored a basket.

"I hear you, man." Pro retrieved the ball and bounce-passed it to me. "But I don't let nobody dis my sister like that. If'n they do, they's gonna hear about it from me, you know? Juvenile or senile or whatever."

It was cold out this early in November. Pro had gloves with the fingers cut off that kept his hands a little warmer than mine. I just shivered and tried to hide my hands inside my coat sleeves. I'd been cold almost all the time lately. Ever since. Ever since the weather changed.

"Libby can . . . " I went up for another shot. " . . . look after herself." The ball missed the sweet spot and barely touched the rim. "Besides, all this stuff about men sticking up for women went out twenty years ago. Didn't you ever hear of women's liberation?"

Pro took a shot from the foul line. Swish. "Lookin' after your family don't got nothin' to do with liberation. It's about respect, man. Respect for you. Respect for your family." He looked at me as I grabbed for the ball, missing it at first go. "What'd you do if somebody bad-mouthed your mother right in front of your face? Smile and look the other way?"

I dribbled the ball a few times, considering the fact that my mother probably received more bad-mouthing from me than from anybody else on this planet. "Didn't you ever hear of turning the other cheek?" I asked him.

"Yeah, Jesus said that. But he was talkin' 'bout himself, not his mother. Nobody ever bad-mouthed Mary, you know. And Jesus could get plenty mad, like what he did to those money-changers, right?"

I drew a blank. For a kid who was supposed to be culturally disadvantaged, Pro knew at least a couple of things I didn't. Of course, my Christian religious education consisted of one old Classic comic book based loosely on the Bible and two Charlton Heston movies shot in fading Technicolor. Thanks to my father, I probably knew more about Gautama Buddha than I did about Jesus.

"Well, it was my father's idea to let him go. Libby was hopping mad. She wanted to string Rug up." I tried a set shot that didn't even come close.

"I think I like your sister."

"Yeah, I kind of like her, too," I said.

There was a funny silence after that. I don't think I'd ever admitted *liking* Libby to any human in my entire life. It wasn't that I actively *disliked* her, or felt disinterested or distant, it was just that I never really thought about it. Maybe in families you don't think about relationships or caring or needing each other until it's too late.

There was a shout from the other side of the fence. "Yo! Pro! You wanna play ball? Little pickup?"

Pro and I looked out at three kids about my size, though probably a year or two younger. I panicked. It was one thing to practice a few shots, just between the two of us. It was something else altogether to risk disgrace at the hands of three strangers.

"Sorry, guys," I said. "We're just, uh, prac—"

Prometheus cut me off and spoke directly to the kid. "Sure, man. 'Bout time we had a real game. We'll take you on two against three."

I stared at him, feeling my poor little heart begin a bass-drum thump inside my chest. "Listen, Pro, I'm not ready —"

"You're ready enough," Pro snapped back.

"No, really —"

"Listen up, Moonkid. A guy who waits around till he thinks he's ready ain't never gonna be ready enough. That's what my old man used to say. Now let's play."

I was still trying to figure out that particular chunk of street wisdom when Pro tossed the ball to our opponents. He gave them a couple minutes to warm up while he tried to clue me in to some of the rules of the game. I confess that most of his words went over my head, or were drowned out by that thumping in my chest, but I did catch something about taking the ball back to half-court after making a basket. As if I might ever make a basket.

Our opponents weren't tall, but they were quick and had good ball sense. The tallest of them seemed to be named Jamal. The other two never got identified, though mentally I named them Red Nikes and Toque after their respective outfits. Jamal had a good set-shot, but his lay-ups weren't going in. Red Nikes didn't like to shoot at all, but he could dribble like crazy. Toque had lots of speed and a lay-up that worked.

To be honest, the basketball observations

above were supplied by Pro, who told me all this as if it would somehow help our game. Exactly what he expected me to do with this information wasn't clear. Nor had we ever played an actual game of basketball before, even against each other. But obviously there was no sense in repeating the fact that I wasn't ready, or might never be ready, or that the whole idea of ready — as in rough 'n ready — might not be part of my mostly-alien personality.

"We'll take it out," Pro declared, as if this were already decided.

He stepped off the edge of the basketball court, looked at the three players on the other side who seemed unaware that the game had begun, and tossed the ball to me.

Now what? I thought. Red Nikes had come to life and was racing towards me, arms up and waving. Jamal had gone over to Pro, blocking a return pass. Toque was under the basket, waiting to block my shot or grab the rebound. Not much I could do but dribble.

I started bouncing the ball, trying to make my way around Red Nikes and closer to the basket, but the kid wouldn't get out of my way. After three or four tries to get in, I simply grabbed the ball and looked around for Pro. He must have seen my problem, and chose that moment to break free of Jamal and race towards the basket.

I bounce-passed the ball to where he was — but

not where he was going. The ball would have gone out, but Toque moved fast to grab it, dribbled twice to take it back, then threw it to Red Nikes who did a set shot that scored. Two-zip for the bad guys.

Pro grabbed the ball and came over beside me before he took it out.

"Sorry," I said.

"No problem," he told me. "Just when I do that, you gotta aim ahead, you know?"

"Yeah, right."

"And try to get in for a basket yourself. That kid on you ain't so hot."

"He kept blocking me," I whined.

"Use your butt, man. Push into him. He'll get out of the way."

"Right," I replied. It seemed to me that I had heard this advice somewhere before.

Pro went out, threw the ball to me and once again I dribbled around, pushing back at my man to get closer to the board. It worked, too. Red Nikes sort of melted back, still harassing me with those hands of his, but I got a chance to move in. Then Pro made his break, I bounce-passed, he grabbed the ball and went for a lay-up. In! Two-two: good guys and bad guys tied up.

Toque took it out for them, tossed the ball to Jamal, who tossed the ball to Red Nikes. I got on him, trying to harass him the same way he'd harried me, with arms and shoulders and the other flailing parts of our bodies that remind us that we really are overgrown chimpanzees. This worked. He passed to Toque who took an easy shot. A miss. The ball bounced off the rim, hit the ground and ended up with Prometheus. He took it back, brought it forward and then bounce-passed it to the strangest of all places — my hands.

"Go for it, Moonkid," Pro shouted.

Why not? I thought. Red Nikes was otherwise occupied; Jamal was nowhere; Toque was back beside the basket. I looked at the basket, quickly remembered the sweet spot, re-aimed at the backboard and shot the ball with both hands.

"Ohmygod!" I said as the ball went in.

"That's cool," Pro said, giving me a high-five.

I was still stunned as the other team took out the ball and brought it into play. In fact, I was stunned throughout the next basket, leaving poor Prometheus to guard three guys at once. This was no mean endeavor on his part, so I had precious little reason to be surprised when the other team sunk the ball and tied up the game again. In fact, I was so busy basking in my own glory — and the amazement of sinking my very first basket ever in a game — that I scarcely noticed.

"Hey, Moonkid," Pro shouted, breaking the spell. "You ready to get in the game again?"

He was grinning at me as he dribbled over to the out-of-bounds line.

The trouble with basketball, of course, is that it

doesn't allow much time for basking in glory, or contemplating the joys of success, or any of the more sedate and meditative aspects of sport. I suspect that golf or croquet might be better for this, because of their slower pace, but basketball is a game with relentless action. Basket, take out, basket, take out, failed shot, back to half-court, basket . . . et cetera, meaning all this gets repeated at length until the players are hot, sweaty and out-of-breath.

In no time, we had all abandoned our jackets and were playing in T-shirts despite the cold. In ten minutes, with the score something like 12-12, I was breathing like a Mack truck trying to pull a load of logs up a mountain. In fifteen minutes, after my third basket, I was too exhausted to hear my own breathing but became aware that my sweat, if it were not evaporating so quickly from my forehead, might otherwise be making puddles on the ground. In twenty minutes, after I missed my third consecutive attempt at a basket, I wanted to call it quits.

"Hey, man, we just got started," said Toque.

"You wanna quit just 'cuz you's ahead," argued Red Nikes.

"They ain't ahead. It's a tie," Jamal pointed out, though incorrectly. Despite the two-on-three odds, Prometheus' lay-up and my feed pass had kept us even. The three baskets I scored had put us ahead.

"No way, man," I said, my voice hoarse.

"It's okay," Pro broke in. "Sudden death, man. Next two baskets in a row take it, okay?"

There was a little grumbling on the other side, but Pro was larger than any of them and had this kind of presence, a bit like Ms. Noble but on a smaller scale. Besides, it was his ball.

"Our out," Pro declared. "Moonkid, you take it."

This was a switch. I stepped into the out-of-bounds, wondering if I'd ever be able to get rid of the ball in the twenty seconds or whatever that's allowed. It turned out to be easier than I thought. Pro lured Jamal down to a spot where he bumped into Toque. Then he broke free, grabbed my pass, dribbled twice and went up into one of the most graceful lay-ups I have ever seen. If the National Ballet were doing a basketball game to Tchaikovsky, their prima ballerina could not have danced a more beautiful shot.

"Yours, man," Pro said to me. "Be ready."

The other guys took it out, Toque tossing to Jamal, Jamal tossing to Red Nikes, me harassing Red Nikes who tossed back to Jamal. But just as Jamal was going up for his shot, Pro somehow got the ball. I still don't know how he did it — some trick with quick hands and a fast turn — but we ended up with the ball in our possession, as they say.

Pro took it back to clear the ball and then tossed it to me.

I was at the end of the key, Red Nikes in front of me, Toque down by the board, Jamal all over Prometheus. And I was tired. Twenty minutes of this had worn me out, exhausted my lungs, made my arms and hands limp. But here was the ball, waiting, and the game, ready to end. Pro was making no effort to get free. It was up to me. I had to find something inside: one last push.

I swore, something we'd heard a lot of from the other team, but a bit surprising coming from me. Then I started dribbling forward, pushing at Red Nikes with my shoulder while Toque came forward to try to steal the ball. No time. I stopped, turned, went up and took a shot. It hit the rim and bounced back, so I grabbed for it. Red Nikes wanted it, but I wanted it more. I grabbed the ball, my hands like claws, then dribbled, stepped once, went up with Toque trying to block, and sent it right at the sweet spot.

Bounce, in.

"Yes!!" I cried. It was probably the only time in my life I ever said something worth two exclamation points.

"You did it, man," Pro said, and then his arm was around me, and mine was around him, and we were like a couple of little kids dancing in the sandbox. The other side was grumbling, the usual accusations of charging, moving foul, steps, and the like, but we didn't care. We'd won the game twice, the second time on a brilliant shot — if you'll pardon my *chutzpah* — by yours truly: Ian Michael Jordan Callisto McNaughton. Definite NBA material, if I do say so myself.

Prometheus walked me to the streetcar line, celebrating our victory along the way. We went over each glorious basket, each successful pass, each wonderful manoeuvre. We demeaned the other kids for their inability to coordinate, the way they couldn't break up our initial pass/lay-up combination, even the way they dressed. We were champions — victors — enjoying the fruits of battle that all conquerors have known since the Greeks stormed out of the wooden horse and captured Troy. Yes!!

So I walked into my house with this most enormous grin, ready to tell somebody, anybody, all about the whole game: detailed play-by-plays, careful recounting of my growing confidence and ability on the court, a verbal reconstruction of each of my four baskets. After all, I was a man of words. What was the point of so spectacular a victory if there was no one to tell?

But the house was dark. I walked to my father's bedroom, peeked past the half-open door and saw him snoring away on the half-inch felt pad he called a mattress. Nine-thirty and he was out for the night. It just shows what serious, bourgeois work can do to you.

So I went down to Libby's room, the smile still up there on my face, cheek-to-cheek. I knocked

lightly on the door, expecting her to yell something foul and then find her bent over one
textbook or another at her desk. But there was no
response. I knocked louder, but still no answer.

I opened the door. "Libby?"

The room was empty. Her desk lamp was on,
glaring onto a set of notes on yellow paper, casting
a duller light on her battered wooden chair, on the
messy bookshelf, on the heaps of clothing under
the window. I could see Muffin, the beaten-up
teddy bear at the corner of her bed. But no Libby.

I lost my smile. I sat down on her bed and
looked at her chair, felt the emptiness crawl into
my heart and turn it into a cold little stone.
"Libby, I was dynamite tonight. You should have
seen me," I said to no one at all. Then I picked up
the stuffed bear. "I was great, really." But Muffin
just stared back in silence.

Chapter 26

My journal #5. Nov. 6

*Played a little basketball last night with Moonkid.
He didn't do too bad when you think how bad he
played a month ago. We played against Rufus and
Jamal and some kid I didn't know. They* ~~wasn't~~
*weren't too tough to beat. But Moonkid did really
good. He didn't fall down like he used to, and he
even got a basket or two. I think it was maybe a
good thing for him to play like that, against some
guys. It'll build up his* ~~confedence~~ *confidence so
maybe he can play some high school kids sometime.*

*Ms. Noble says that I'm doing really good in
school. She say that my reading is better. I'm*

almost up to "grade level," that's what she said. I thought she said "grade eleven" but turns out that grade level just means I'm like everybody else in grade 7. I said Moonkid was helping me and she gave me this ~~froun~~ ~~frown~~ funny look. She ~~got~~ has something against Moonkid, I guess. When I go to high school, Ms. Noble says she might ~~recmend~~ ~~reccomend~~ recommend me to be in the advanced grade 9 class. She says I'm really pretty smart. I said, I could of have told you that.

Next week there's this eclipse (how you like that good spelling?) coming up. That's where a shadow goes across the moon. Anyway, some ~~astra~~ astronomy club is doing a Moon Party way on the edge of town. Moonkid read something in the paper and I said we ~~outta~~ ought to go. It could be cool, watching an eclipse through a ~~telaco~~ telescope. Wish we could take Amos, but its too late at night for him.

Checked out that thing with Mount Olympus. It's a cheapo triple bill up in Woodside — no WWF thing, just some little ~~prompter~~ promoter put it together. Mount Olympus is doing his comeback match against some guy called The Crusher. There's also gonna be this tag team with the Canucks against some team I never heard of. Then the title match, Jack Flash vs. Okimoto. I think maybe I oughtta go. I ain't seen my dad in a couple years, so at least I know he's still alive. Guess he's still wrestling, too, but it's ~~gotta~~ got to be

hard for an old man over 30. Might be ~~easyer~~
easier if Moonkid came along, but he's kind of
~~werid~~ ~~wierd~~ *funny about family stuff.*

*That's all for now. Tina's come back home. Don't
know if that's a good thing or not. Says she's got a
real boyfriend and cleaned up her act now. I think
I heard that line before. Guess we'll see.*

Chapter 27

"I didn't know buses came out this far," I said to Prometheus, as we bounced along on ours, a number 52B Ellesmere which had already deposited all of its passengers except us.

"All you gotta do is call bus info'mation, they'll tell you how to get anyplace. Got no choice if you don't got a car."

"So if you're such a transportation genius, how do we get back?"

"Last bus is 11:07 p.m. No problem," he announced. "How long you lived in the city, anyway?"

"Obviously not long enough," I muttered.

Prometheus ignored my irritated, if not depressed, mood and continued to stare out the window. We had left most of the city behind a few minutes ago, so now we were passing fields, widely-spaced farm houses, and the occasional barking dog. It reminded me of when we lived out in the country, in Mt. Forest, a spot so godforsaken in my memories that I shudder at the mere passing recollection of it.

The bus driver put on the brakes and brought the bus to a stop, essentially in the middle of nowhere. Then he turned to us. "This is your stop, boys."

I looked around. We were at the bottom of a driveway, five hundred yards from an unlighted farmhouse and barn, with nothing around us but fields, a broken mailbox and three trees *sans* leaves. "This is *it*?" I said, italicizing the it as best I could with vocal chords.

"Two stops past Miller Sideroad," the driver said. "This is it."

There was no time to think. The driver didn't look particularly mischievous. He had that basic bus driver face — small chin, bushy eyebrows, protruding nasal hair — that inspires a certain amount of confidence. And Prometheus was already at the door, waiting for me to join him.

We stepped into the cold dark night and then watched as the bus disappeared down the road.

"Good thing we got the moon," Prometheus said, which was true. The full moon hung up in the sky like the forty-watt bulb that tries vainly to illuminate my blue-painted bedroom. As my eyes slowly adapted, the moonlight revealed a certain undulous shape in the fields that surrounded us and showed us the driveway that led to a house. A dog barked in the distance, and I jumped. Ever since a particularly unpleasant run-in with a Bull Terrier in grade six, I have regarded dogs with a respect bordering on terror.

"And look at those stars, man. Don't think I ever saw so many stars."

I looked up from the dog-infested landscape to the dark sky above it. The stars dusted the sky like celestial dandruff — no, that's too cynical — the stars looked like somebody had spilled white carpet cleaner all over black carpet — no, the stars —

"It's like you're lookin' at the face of God, eh?" Prometheus said, solving my simile problem.

"I guess," I grunted, none too cheery. I could feel the cold seeping into my jacket and under my watchman's toque. "Are you sure this is the right place? There aren't even any lights on."

"The guy said they turn off all the lights," Prometheus told me, since he had made the phone call to set this up. "Said we should look for a bunch of red flashlights."

"Right," I said, sarcastically. "Red flashlights." Now I was certain we were stranded in the middle of nowhere, about to be set upon by barking dogs, our bodies then frozen until the spring thaw.

We stumbled down the driveway in a phosphorescent half-darkness. A farmhouse loomed up ahead, a kind of Victorian gothic monster that belonged in a Stephen King novel, and a barn that looked appropriate for murder, suicide and rotting bodies. But back behind the barn, there they were — twenty people walking around, all of them carrying red flashlights.

"Told you I got the right place," Prometheus announced, probably smiling, but it was hard to tell. "Guy says they use red flashlights so they can see better in the dark."

"I knew that," I lied.

We walked up to the first telescope, where three men and one older woman were standing around. The men were your basic middle-aged types: layers of sweatshirts covering oversized bellies, various styles of baseball caps on their heads, an assortment of beards, goatees and mustaches decorating their faces. They did not, in any way, look like rocket scientists. The woman, on the other hand, had a certain Roberta Bondar quality: shining grey hair, a strong nose, an air of assurance that suggested experience at NASA headquarters.

"Ah, two more," she said as we walked up. "I'm Betty Millar, with the Astronomical Society. You are?"

"Uh, Ian. Ian McNaughton," I said, and she nodded.

"Pro. I mean, Prometheus Gibbs. I'm the

guy who called. Ian's my friend."

There was a little pause. It took a while for
Pro's name to sink in with the adults. It took a
while for the phrase "Ian's my friend" to sink in
with me. I don't think, in my entire life up to that
momentous moment, that any human being had
ever described himself as my friend. I mean, it
would have been the social kiss of death in any
school I'd ever attended. Of course I have acquain-
tances, a sister, various other relatives, neighbors
and fellow students, but even R.T. was more of an
admirer than a friend.

For a long time, I decided that my dearth of
social relationships was more than adequately
explained by the simple fact that I was a visiting
alien. What, after all, did I have in common with
earthlings? But now Pro was my friend, or willing
to call himself that, and he was very definitely an
earthling. So much for theories.

"Ah, Prometheus," Mrs. Millar said. "Probably
the only Greek god who doesn't have a constellation named after him. Of course he was an outlaw,
the god who gave fire to us humans, and all.
Anyway, this is Steven and Steven, maybe we'll
make that Steven One and Steven Two, just to
simplify, and a person who's just joined us, uh —"

"Robert Dietz," threw in the non-Steven. He
was wearing a leather jacket that looked more
expensive than the outfits of the two Stevens put
together, and he carried a camera with a lens so

long it could have been used as a club. "When's the eclipse, exactly?"

Mrs. Millar looked at her watch. "Forty-two minutes. I'm sure you can watch it through any of the members' telescopes, but there's much to see before that happens. Now, Steven One is our vice-president in charge of new members."

Steven One smiled, revealing a fair amount of gold and silver dental work. "Nice to see y'all," he said in a kind of drawl. "Get lots of new folk out here for things like the eclipse, but if yer interested, we meet once a month, the first Wednesday after the new moon. Best thing to bring is binoculars like Steven here, a lawn chair and some coffee, because it gets damn cold in the winter. But you might just get hooked anyhow. Like I say, star gazing's the most fun you can have outdoors with yer clothes on." He grinned again, then looked a bit sheepish. "Sorry, Betty."

She shrugged. "Why not show them Saturn and explain how all this works?" And then she went off to meet with some of the other stargazers.

Steven One took on his assignment quite readily. "This here's a five-inch apochromatic refractor," he said, referring to the telescope beside him. Though none of us knew the meaning of apochromatic, nobody stopped him from going on. "I've got a two-inch lens on it, so we're looking at seventy power or thereabouts. When you set up a scope like this, you put the mount on a polar alignment, so this here leg points north, and then you can adjust the tracking with a motor or just these two knobs here. You got all that?"

"Maybe a little slower," Prometheus said.

"Okay," said Steven One, smiling again. "The whole problem here is that the earth rotates, you know, around its axis and around the sun. So you get your scope set up on something like Saturn, and it keeps moving away on you because of the earth turning and rotating, see. So to get around that, you set up towards the north pole, and then this here equatorial mount takes care of the rest. It's just to get things to sit still so you can look at 'em."

"I got it now," Prometheus said, though I wasn't sure he was speaking for all of us — certainly not for me.

"How much does a unit like this cost?" asked Dietz, admiring the telescope more than the stars over our heads.

"About four thousand, new. It all depends on the optics and the finder and the quality of the mount. I got this for about fourteen hundred, but the mount's too small so there's a lot of jiggle, you know?" He bent down and looked into the scope, then adjusted a couple of knobs. "Anyway, there's Saturn. You can see the rings fairly well, and if you look real close you can see two of the moons."

Dietz got to the scope first and peered into it. "Yeah, I see it. But no moons. Where's the moons?" he asked, still not surrendering his spot.

"You got to do a trick with yer eyes," Steven One explained. "You look a little bit off, not right at Saturn, just a bit off, and you'll see Triton up at about the two o'clock position."

Dietz bent back down, squinted, but got up obviously dissatisfied. "Still can't see it."

"Let me try," Steven Two said, and certainly it was someone else's turn. He bent forward and looked through the lens. "Wow, how about that?" he said, talking to the scope, apparently. "How come it's all white?"

"Oh, you can see color sometimes," Steven One told him. "Depends on the sky. We got a little too much mist tonight, turns everything white."

Prometheus went up to the scope and took his turn, but said nothing. He motioned for me to come after him, which I did. The metal ring of the telescope lens felt cold, but the view was clear enough: Saturn, a glowing ball with a belly-band of rings. I watched for a while, then tried to see the moons — and maybe I did, up at two o'clock, glowing brighter than the stars behind.

"Pretty cool, eh?" Pro asked.

"Pretty cool," I agreed.

Steven One took over and reset the telescope straight up, fiddled with the knobs, then invited us to look at a cluster of stars called the Pleiades. He said these were relatively new stars, only a hundred million years old, and that there were other stars in the galaxy still forming. The rest of us took our turns looking, Prometheus curious about how the new stars were being formed, Steven Two relatively quiet, and Dietz looking bored.

Finally Steven One aimed the telescope at the moon, which already seemed about five times bigger than it was in the city. Our eyes had become "dark adapted," as Steven One said, so we could see far more than we usually did on a city street or even stepping out of a country house. He slipped a less powerful lens onto the telescope, so we could see the whole moon, and then invited us to take turns looking. Meanwhile, he talked about the moon like a travel guide on a tour bus: mountains, craters, plains, seas, all with names and descriptions. This time I looked through the telescope before Prometheus. After he had finished, there was a major smile on his face.

"No cheese, man," he said.

"Nobody moving, either," I pointed out.

"Maybe you're not a real Moonkid after all."

I shook my head. "Wrong moon."

Dietz asked if he could take a picture, something that involved changing lenses and hooking some other device onto his camera. I wondered why he brought such an enormous telephoto lens if all he really wanted was to bum some time on a telescope, but decided not to ask.

Prometheus and I took the fifteen minutes or so before the eclipse to wander among the other amateur astronomers. They were an odd crew, mostly the kind of people you'd see selling shoes or behind the counter in a variety store. Occasionally, there was the face of a mad scientist — a crazy guy with beady glasses, a very intent woman busy scribbling notes in a book — but mostly they were ordinary people with an extraordinary dream. I could understand about that.

At nine-thirty, there was a sudden buzz of activity from the amateur astronomers. Steven One came over and urged us to join him at his telescope because the eclipse was about to begin. Steven Two was already there, peering through the eyepiece, while Robert Dietz had managed to get his camera stuck on the end of somebody else's telescope and was busy looking up with a pair of borrowed binoculars.

Right on schedule, at 9:33:20, there was a slight darkening at the edge of the moon. You could see it through the binoculars that Steven Two lent us and you could see it even better through Steven One's telescope. Gradually the darkening took a shape, a black circle, bigger than the moon itself. The shadow of earth.

"Look at that, man," Prometheus said.

Which I did. The shadow of earth crept over the surface of the moon, darkening seas, mountains, volcanoes, everything. In ancient times, it must have been a terrifying thing watching the moon suddenly go black for no reason, everyone wondering if it would ever shine again.

Steven One was going on at length about some technical items having to do with the duration of the eclipse, the shape of the earth's shadow, the way this particular eclipse compared to others he had seen. I don't think either Prometheus or I was paying much attention to him. Compared to the eclipse itself, the magic of the blackening moon, Steven One's science had little appeal.

"That's it," Steven cried out. "That's totality."

What a word. He made it sound like the moon was suddenly dead, or extinct, but all he meant was that the moment of total eclipse had arrived. The moon was dark — well, not entirely dark, especially through the telescope, but very definitely in shadow. It was an eerie sight, really. Even though I knew all about the science and what was really happening, there was still a scary feeling that maybe this time it wouldn't work, that the moon wouldn't ever light up again. No wonder the whole group fell silent: a sudden awe, a prehistoric fear.

"What you thinking about?" Pro asked me.

"Stars," I said, my breath making clouds in the cold. "How big the universe is."

"Me, too," he said.

We were looking up at a night sky with a million stars. People name the stars after ancient gods. Lately, they've taken to sticking numbers on the newest ones because they've run out of names.

Or maybe they believe more in numbers than in names. All of it, the naming, the numbers, is because we're scared, I think, about that immense universe up there.

"You think we count much in all this?" I asked Pro.

"Yeah," Pro said. "I think everything counts, 'cuz of God. We're here to do something. You, me, even that photographer-guy. So maybe we don't seem like much down here with all that up there, but God put us here for something."

"What if you don't believe in God?"

"Then you gotta figure out some other reason for all this. God's the way it makes sense to me. You ever stop to think about the other kind of eclipse, the one where the sun goes all black? You ever stop to think that the moon is 'zactly the right size to block out the sun — not too big, not too small, not too far away — 'zactly the right size? You think that's some kinda accident?"

"What else could it be?" I said.

"It's a plan, man. It's God's plan. Up there, those play-a-deecee stars, there's new stars being born. We stand here and there's new stars being born and we won't know about it for a million years and maybe by then they'll have planets with people like us looking at Earth —"

"And we'll be a supernova," I threw in.

"Yeah, we'll be exploded and they'll see this flash of light and wonder what that means. And what it'll mean is that our turn's over and God's plan is working for somebody else. But we still got our turn, you know. And our turn, that's now."

"Wish I could believe that," I muttered.

"So why don't you?" Pro asked. I could tell he was looking at me, but I kept my eyes on the stars. "You got all this stuff up in your head, so you forget you gotta feel with your heart. Sometimes I think your big brain just gets in the way. You got stuff that's bugging you in your heart, not your head. Stuff like your sister."

I didn't say anything. It was very quiet in the moon-lost dark, not even a wind to stir the damp air.

"Your sister's gonna go away and it's been chewing you up for weeks but you never even told her you gonna miss her. And your momma comes to town and you come over to play ball so you don't even go have dinner with her till I give you a hard time. It's like you got a load of ce-ment around your heart, you know?"

This was getting a little too close for comfort. "Shields on full power, Mr. Scott."

Pro smiled. I could see him, even if he didn't want me to. "See what I mean. Try to talk serious and you gotta make a joke. You're too smart for yourself. You're like that Dr. Spock guy."

"You mean Mr. Spock," I corrected.

"Yeah, the guy with the ears. Come to think of it, you both got funny ears. And you both got the same problem. You can't figure out what to do with the rest of us humans."

"Yeah? How do you know?"

"Cuz maybe I got a little bit of that problem too. Lotta kids say I'm kinda stuck-up. Don't know for sure — maybe it's true. Sure don't got a lotta friends."

"Maybe it's because you're too cool," I suggested.

"Yeah, way cool. Just like you, Moonkid."

The two of us became quiet, thinking not so much about the stars as about ourselves. Fortunately, the edge of the moon reappeared and there was a general sigh from the group that broke the silence.

"The moon's coming back, Moonkid," Prometheus said.

"Good thing," I replied. By now my neck was hurting from staring first up at the sky and then down at the telescope eyepiece. The cold and damp were also getting to my bones.

"You kids enjoy the show?" Steven One asked, tromping over to where we stood near the barn.

"Yeah," Prometheus replied. "It was really something. Thanks for letting us look in your scope."

"No problem. Come back next month. We're going to be looking at a radiant from Orion."

"What's that?" I asked.

"A meteor shower," Steven One explained. "We sometimes get two or three in an hour."

"Cool," Prometheus declared. "We'll be here."

I looked at him, wondering if I really wanted to deal with minus-fifteen January temperatures on the off-chance of seeing a meteor or two. But it seemed the wrong time to say anything.

Prometheus checked his watch and the two of us began walking back down the driveway to the road. The 11:07 bus was scheduled to arrive in five minutes, and actually appeared only three minutes late — good thing, too, judging by the chattering of my teeth.

The same driver, recognizable by his eyebrows and nasal hair, was behind the wheel. He asked us if we "enjoyed" the eclipse, which I thought was a funny word to use, as if an eclipse were like a movie or a play and somehow subject to human appraisal. But Prometheus told him it was "cool," and that seemed to settle the matter. We walked down the aisle and took seats opposite the rear door, just over the heating vent.

For five minutes or so we rode in silence. Maybe our jaws were still frozen from the two hours we'd spent in an icy field, or maybe whatever we had to say seemed pretty insignificant compared to what we had seen. But finally we thawed out, and Prometheus spoke to me.

"Moonkid?" he asked, looking out the window rather than in my direction.

"Yeah?"

"I got something to ask you. Kind of a favor."

"Like what? I've only got two bucks in my pocket," I said, cynically.

"Not that kind," he said. "It's sort of like what we were talking about before. I got this guy I've gotta go see and I'd kind of like you along."

"Me?"

"Yeah. Next Saturday. It's a wrestling thing out in Woodside."

"Wrestling?"

"Look, I don't wanna explain. I just wondered if maybe you'd come. For the company, you know?"

I could see Prometheus' face reflected in the window glass of the bus. He had a funny look, some mix of anticipation and regret and embarrassment. I had a hunch he'd really rather go to this wrestling match on his own, but for some reason it was important to have me along.

"You writing this up for school, or your journal or something?"

"Yeah, kind of."

"Kind of what?" I asked him.

"Kind of personal. Kind of like the moon thing. Kind of like a lot of things. Look, you gonna come or what?" Pro still wasn't looking at me.

"Yeah, sure I'm going to come along." I paused for a second. "I'm your friend, aren't I?"

Pro smiled and turned to me. "Yeah, man. You're my best bud."

What could I do but smile back. First time ever I was somebody's *best* bud.

Chapter 28

My journal #6. Nov 21

~~Been~~ It's been a long time since I wrote in this journal much. Sorry journal. Ms. Noble's been giving me so much homework I don't ~~got~~ have ~~no~~ any time to write to you. That ~~don't~~ doesn't mean I ~~aint~~ haven't been thinking any, but I don't have ~~no~~ any time to write all the stuff in my brain down on paper.

Ms. Noble's been giving me all kind of books to read now that I read so ~~good~~ well. I read Count of Mountie Cristo and Tale of Two ~~Citys~~ Cities, *not* the ~~orige~~ originals (had to look that word up), but kind of short books. I also read all the stories in my reading book. Moonkid didn't help me ~~none~~ ~~any~~ with any of that stuff. He thinks these books are kind of old ~~fashend~~ fashioned for somebody to read these days. But I like the stories. I told him, "They're cool, Moonkid. Maybe you should broaden your reading a little." Well, that got him. I saw Moonkid's jaw drop so far it looked like it might fall right off his face.

Moonkid brought me a good book too. It's called Snowbound and I like it. I asked him if there ~~be are~~ were any story books about wrestling, but he didn't know ~~none~~ any. Instead he got me this book called The Contender, it's about boxing. I guess that's close. I've been trying to write book reports for Ms. Noble, but they're still hard. My spelling stinks. I asked Moonkid how come I can read ~~better~~ so fast and I still can't spell good. He said that my reading just needed ~~confe~~ confidence but spelling takes lots of practice. So I got this spelling book to practice words, but it seems kind of dumb.

I think my dad would be proud if he knew how good I was doing. Don't know why I should care though. It's funny how I feel about him. Sometimes I think I hate him because he used to beat on Mama and Tina and me. But sometimes I miss him. How come I don't just feel one thing? Maybe I should ask Moonkid, but he ~~don't~~ doesn't know much about people. He's better with books and stars and all that.

I never did write about that night Moonkid and ~~me~~ I went to see the eclipse. It was cool, looking at the stars close up through a telescope. Makes you feel kind of small in the big universe up there. Makes you wonder, if we're so small and ~~insig~~ insignificant, how come we got so much time to fight each other. Moonkid thinks there ~~be~~ is something wrong with people. Me, I don't know. Anyway, we're going to another one after Christmas so maybe I'll write about that.

I thought things were going pretty good for a while lately, like God was ~~gonna~~ going to start smiling down on me a little more regular like. Moonkid's getting almost good at basketball and Amos ~~aint~~ isn't getting beat up so much at school and Tina's been straight for three weeks now. Then Mr. Donaldson at the school called my mama and said there was a big meeting tomorrow and she had to come. I guess I'm in some kind of trouble, but Ms. Noble won't say ~~nothing~~ anything about it. Guess I'll find out what I did wrong when I go to the meeting. Too bad, because everything else is pretty good. Moonkid even said he'd go to Mount Olympus's wrestling match with me, but I still didn't tell him it's my dad wrestling. Maybe I will, maybe I won't. Got to think more about that.

Chapter 29

I was in math class, chewing on my pencil, hoping that the pencil shavings lodged between my teeth wouldn't some day be identified as carcinogens, when the P.A. went off.

"Mr. Swayze?" came the crackling voice. I've always suspected that this inquiry comes first to make sure the teacher referred to is actually awake and alive before proceeding.

"Yes," answered Swayze gruffly. He was busy working on a lesson plan for some other class. As far as I could tell, he had never developed a lesson plan of any kind for us.

"Is Ian McNaughton in class?"

Swayze looked up and saw me chewing away. "Yes, in body. I can't answer for the location of his mind."

This witticism was lost on the secretary downstairs and on most of the rest of the class. Only Bronson laughed, and he was probably stoned because it was the period just after lunch.

"Would you ask him to stop by the office at the end of the day, please? It's important."

Swayze looked up at the P.A. speaker as if it were the only thing within shouting distance worth conversing with. "Are you sure you don't want him now? Of course, all of us will miss him . . . "

The pause was for sarcastic impact . . . and it worked. The whole class laughed, inspired by the drug-induced hooting of Bronson, now amplified by laughter from Shannon, Joel, Chris and John Dunstable et al. When Ronnie noticed the rest of them laughing, he started as well, though I doubt he knew what it was all about.

"No, the end of the day will be fine," the secretary concluded, then signed off with a crackle of static.

"Well, Ian, it looks like you're in trouble again," Mr. Swayze observed dryly.

"'Cuz of his big mouth — or maybe his ears," shouted Bronson, and that dissolved everyone in laughter one more time. Then some began a rhythmical chant of "Moonkid . . . Moonkid . . . Moonkid." This was sufficient to annoy Mr. Swayze, who quickly cut it off and demanded we get back to our workbooks.

I opened mine and began working on a list of

adjectives to describe Bronson, a list which kept me occupied the rest of the period: *armpit sludge, nasal mutant, phlegm wad, waste of DNA, pimple festering on the butt of life, puke breath, belly-button crusty, plaque eater, phlegm chunk* . . . My list was lengthy and finally concluded with *bubonic dog scrotum* which had the appropriate scientific, historical, biological and scatological impact.

Working on the list kept my mind off the major problem — why did they want me in the office? Was there some new problem with my spare period, or had Ms. Noble complained directly to Mrs. Greer? Or was it all over and Greer was going to transfer me to Markdale?

After school, I trudged up to the office on the third floor, and waited at the counter while the secretaries kept busily hanging Christmas tree ornaments on the most pathetic synthetic tree I had ever seen. Finally I uttered my very loudest *ahem*, got the attention of the dark-haired secretary known as Wanda the Wicked Witch, and announced my name.

"Why are you here?" she asked.

"Don't know," I replied. "I must have done something." I shrugged. *Mea culpa. Mea maxima culpa.* In school and in religion, aren't we always guilty?

"I'll check with Mrs. Greer," she said, picking up the phone.

A minute later, Mrs. Greer appeared in the

hallway that led to her office. I tried to stay calm.
She didn't look angry, at least. Maybe I could talk
my way out of whatever I'd done. Maybe I could
make one more deal.

"Ian," she said, smiling.

"Yes'm," I said. "Look, I'm sorry. I didn't mean
it," I began.

"Sorry for what?"

"Whatever I did."

"What did you do?"

I realized that I was in the middle of a hopelessly stupid conversation. It's a funny feeling,
when two people are talking and it *seems* like
they're talking to each other but neither one
knows what the other is talking about. Kind of
faux conversation.

"So I didn't do anything?" I asked, my voice
rising.

"Well, I guess you did. But nothing bad," Mrs.
Greer said simply.

Wanda, the wicked secretarial witch, was looking back and forth at us as if one or the other or
both had lost our minds. Finally she shook her head
and went back to staring at her computer screen.

"So why was I supposed to come here?"

"Because you have a visitor, Ian," Mrs. Greer
announced. "She's down in Mr. Dinnerstein's office
in guidance."

So I walked through the connecting door to the
guidance office, stopping at the second cubicle

where Mr. Dinnerstein would usually have been sitting with his feet propped on the desk. But Mr. Dinnerstein's desk was empty. My visitor was sitting — no, that's too small a word — occupying a wooden armchair.

It was Ms. Noble.

She looked up when I came to the doorway. "Ian, I'm so glad you could see me," Ms. Noble said, as if I had any real choice in the matter. There was a smile that played around her lips. Whether it was a real smile or one of the gritted-teeth variety, I couldn't say. "Close the door, please."

I did as asked. I immediately felt cowed by her presence — no, I'll change words again, because even cows manage a certain amount of self-respect — I felt sheeped.

"Please sit down," Ms. Noble said, offering me the swivelling seat that was usually occupied by Mr. Dinnerstein.

I sat. So far, I'd followed two orders without saying a word. *This is pathetic*, I said to myself. *You've got to say something.* "Ms. Noble," I began, "uh . . . what brings you . . . here?" I sounded like my intelligence was only slightly beyond the "can mostly control his drooling" level.

"I think you and I have a few things to say to each other," she told me, locking her eyes on mine so that I had little choice but to look away. "For *clarity*."

"Charity?" I said. Even my ears weren't

working properly.

"*Clarity*," she repeated. "When you and I last saw each other, the situation was, shall we say, acrimonious?"

"That might be a good word," I agreed. I believe I was sweating, inordinately, since the guidance cubicle was always quite chilly.

Ms. Noble moved slightly in her chair, a motion which caused the various folds of her flesh and clothing to shift. "Well, let me begin by saying that I do appreciate the tutoring you've been doing for Prometheus. His progress has been really extraordinary and I think much of the credit for that belongs to you."

"Well, really —" I began, but she wasn't finished, and wasn't about to stop for me.

"And to Prometheus himself, who is quite a remarkable young man. He has his limitations, of course, as we all do, but in terms of character and deportment and initiative, we are looking at a truly *remarkable* young man."

"I agree."

"Where we *dis*agree," Ms. Noble went on, fixing my eyes again before I averted my gaze, "is in method and substance. *Rumblefish*, for instance, is —"

"A very good book." The words just jumped out of my mouth, surprising me, astonishing Ms. Noble. Perhaps no one had cut off one of her sentences in her entire life.

"A good-enough book," she corrected, "but hardly great literature. Perhaps it was something that would catch his interest at a certain stage, perhaps it pandered to some adolescent feelings —"

"I think *pandered* is a bit strong," I said, cutting her off again. This was starting to feel good, like a wrestling match where suddenly you find a hold that works.

"I have strong *views*, Ian, as you may have noticed." Ms. Noble let a silence fall, so that the screeching noise from the fluorescent light became all that filled the tiny room. "I happen to believe in the capacity of my students to read *great* literature, and appreciate *great* art, and become part of the world of culture and sophistication and power that has been *denied* them by too many well-meaning people who are content to . . . " She paused to look for a word. " . . . to *pander* to these students as if they were capable of nothing better. Well, they are capable, Ian, and I will not pander."

There was no way I could start to argue with all that, so I asked a simple question. "You think I do?"

She studied my face. "I wasn't sure about you, at first. You'll have to excuse me for turning you into a stereotype, but I've been teaching for twenty-eight years and I have seen many, *many* well-meaning tutors and teachers come . . . and go, while I continue my work with these young people. And I know who profits from those *convenient* and temporary tutoring arrangements. It's not really the child from those projects across from the school. No, it's the nice white boy who gets approval from his parents, a period off from school and a wonderful extra-curricular activity to put on his university scholarship application. And when he's gone off, those of us who *truly* care and *truly* believe in the children, we're left to carry on. Do you understand, this is not a *charity* for me, Ian, this is my life's work?"

"Yes'm," I said, using the word so many revert to with Ms. Noble. But I truly did understand something. I could see where her power came from — her *zeal*, to use that religious word — and it had to do with the same kind of faith that was in Prometheus, something deep and powerful. I was envious. "I'm . . . I'm sorry if I undermined that. I don't think I —"

"Ian, there's nothing to be sorry about," Ms. Noble went on. "I have my methods, which strike some as old-fashioned and I have my standards, which aren't even politically correct any more, but I get a great deal from my students because I believe in them."

I nodded.

"And so do you, or at least you have done from Prometheus. You gave him confidence. You instilled some rigor. You even got him looking up words in the dictionary. You succeeded where I couldn't and I . . . I admire that." There was another pause. I wondered whether her words of admiration were galling her, or whether she just had trouble finding the right ones. Finally, she went on. "I realize now that I underestimated you."

"You did?"

"I did. I assumed you were one of those others, the young people who drop in for a while, make a little trouble for the child and his teacher, and then go off to the next charity. I thought that when you were forbidden to use the school, you'd be off like the breeze. But you weren't like that. You didn't just give up on Prometheus. The two of you formed a better alliance outside of school than you could ever have formed inside it."

"Yeah, he's taught me a lot," I said.

"And you've taught him a great deal," Ms. Noble went on. "So if I say to you now that you're free to come back into the school and do tutoring there, does it matter much?"

"No, not much. It might be better on some days," I told her, "but we've been playing some basketball, too, and the apartment is okay except for the TV noise. I guess I better check with Pro."

"He said that he wanted to check with you. I'll leave the matter in your hands. That's a fair deal of *trust* I'm placing in you, Ian. I hope you won't abuse it."

"No, ma'am," I said. Was I blushing? Why can't I control my skin at times like this?

"Prometheus is a young man who has *suffered* a fair amount of upset and rejection in his life, Ian.

I was afraid you were going to be one more person to show up in his life and then *disappear*, but there was a part of you I couldn't see when I first met you, and it's taken you and Prometheus a long way."

"What was that?" I asked her.

"Your heart, Ian," she said, smiling at me, this time in a genuine way. "Try as you might to hide it, you have a very big heart."

I do? I thought. *You're crazy*! I thought. *I'm an alien from some other planet and I'm just visiting here and I don't care about earth or humans or anybody*. But I kept my mouth shut, because it was the wrong moment to speak back to Ms. Noble who had said so many very nice things about me, and who was obviously placing a fair amount of faith in this funny-looking white boy. And maybe she was right. Maybe I had a much bigger heart than any self-respecting alien from Alpha Centauri has any reason to have.

Chapter 30

My journal #7. November 23

That big meeting at school was kind of funny. I was ~~worryed~~ worried that I did something wrong, but it wasn't me that did it. It was Ms. Noble. Looks like I got her in ~~alot~~ a lot of trouble.

I went down to this meeting in Mr. Donaldson's ~~offise~~ office after school today, and my mama had to come to it too. So my mama was sitting outside the office on a bench, like she was sent down by a teacher or something, and I didn't like that much. Anyway, when I got there we went into Mr. Donaldson's office and it was really crowded with all these people from the board of education. There was this ~~superten~~ ~~superintend~~ superintendent and a couple ~~consultents~~ consultants (how come I always got to look up the words for these educa-tion guys?) and some black guy called the race relations co-something and Mr. Donaldson and a VP and a teacher union guy and Ms. Noble. Everybody was all dressed up except my mom and me. It felt like we should ~~of~~ have put on our church clothes, like it was a wedding or a ~~funaral~~ funeral or like that.

And you know what it was all about? My let-ter!! That letter I wrote to the board of education back in October when they kicked Moonkid out of the school. It ~~werent~~ wasn't even a good letter. One guy showed it to me and I could see all the spelling ~~misstakes~~ mistakes. I guess I was so mad I didn't even use the ~~dictionery~~ dictionary.

Anyway, these suit guys started asking me all sorts of questions, like was I happy in class and how was the ~~tutorring~~ tutoring how did I like being tutored and did I have any ~~complancts~~ complaints about Ms. Noble? So I told them that Ms. Noble was a great teacher, and most of the time I like her okay, but ~~her~~ she and Mr. Donaldson got me mad when they kicked out Moonkid. Then the race relations co-something guy asked if I felt ~~dis~~ ~~discrimn~~ discriminated (who came up with all these big words, anyway?) against by Ms. Noble or Mr. Donaldson. I said, how can I be discriminated against if they're black and I'm black too, unless maybe they got something against kids with big feet. Then every-

body laughed and they asked mama a couple questions.

Ms. Noble had some stuff to say about my good progress and how the tutoring was a good thing but it took too much time out of class. Then the suits talked about some kind of interplanetary (was that the word?) cooperation and some special kind of development and a whole bunch of stuff I didn't quite get. Anyway, when it was all over they said that ~~Moonkid~~ Ian (I got to start using his real name) could do the tutoring in school if we both still wanted to, and I said I didn't know because we did tutoring and played basketball and couldn't do both of those things in the school ~~libary~~ library. Ms. Noble said she'd go to talk to Ian and my mama said she was real happy with how it was all going. And I said I was glad that somebody read my letter and took it ~~serious~~ seriously.

After, I told Ms. Noble I was sorry about all the trouble, but she said don't worry about it ~~none~~ any. She said I should always stick up for myself when I think I'm right. So I did, and I'm glad. Mama said she was proud of me. I bet my old man would be proud too, but that's another story. I guess I'll write about that next time.

Chapter 31

In gym class the next day, we had a supply teacher. He announced Fred's absence to loud general cheering. After attendance, he proceeded to toss out a half-dozen basketballs, suggesting that we amuse ourselves with our balls, as it were, while he retreated to the relative safety of the gym office.

Bedlam. Twenty boys with six basketballs and no supervising adult is almost as disastrous as equal numbers of dogs and cats in a single kennel. Within minutes, I had been hit twice in the head, Trevor had been assaulted both above and below the belt, Willie had managed to stuff two balls under his T-shirt for a Dolly Parton look, and Skye had taken off to the locker room with the one relatively new basketball, probably for future resale.

But even chaos loses its appeal after a while, and eventually the dominant males settled down into groups under the two far-end baskets. At the south end of the gym, they started playing twenty-one, and at the north end, a half-court game of basketball began. A few of us Feebs, a general term of derision based on *feeble* and usually reserved for Trevor, Willie and me, had retreated to the sidelines during the melee. We stayed there as organized sport was reinvented and civilization slowly restored.

Eventually, the Feebs drifted to the north end, less out of interest in the game than out of self-defense. The guys playing twenty-one were shooting so wildly and with so many balls that anyone standing nearby was in danger of receiving a ball or two in the face. The half-court teams were at least organized. One was under the leadership of Ryan, the reigning class athlete. The other was captained by Josh whose sheer physical mass out-weighed the fact that he couldn't run, shoot or dribble.

Ryan's team was clobbering Josh's. They were boosted by the ability to shoot, a vague sense of team play, and an aggressiveness that knew no limits, except that after too many fouls, Josh would yell out, "Hey, clean it up," with enough threat to bring the game back within the bounds of fair play. Nonetheless, Josh's side was losing badly and Ryan was crowing about his general excellence as a basketball player and/or human being.

"Use a fast break," I hollered out at this point. My suggestion was meant to be helpful.

"A fast break?" Josh said, staring at me, his ordinary good humor somewhat strained by a score of a zillion to two against his team. "What do you know about a fast break, Moonkid?"

"Well, not much," I admitted. Prometheus had only begun to tell me about team tactics, breaks, screens, weaves and all the other manoeuvres that make basketball look like diagrams for a Balanchine ballet. "But it might help."

Ryan held the ball on the sidelines and laughed. "You guys in that much trouble that you gotta go to Moonkid for advice?" Ryan's team joined him in laughter.

"I didn't ask for advice," Josh said angrily. "Moonkid yelled it at me."

"I was just saying —" I began, but no one was listening.

"Well, we all know what an athlete Moonkid is, don't we?" Ryan said, bringing more laughter, even from Josh. "So Moonkid, why don't you put your body where your mouth is? Why don't you just *show* these guys how to do a fast break?"

By now, half the people in the gym were staring at me. I tried to back off. "The sides won't be even," I pointed out.

"Yeah, if we give you to one side, we've gotta

take two guys away from the other," Ryan declared. It took a little time for that witticism to sink in, but then it brought more laughter.

As Prometheus would say, it was time to put up or shut up. I decided on the former. "Okay," I said, "how about Trevor and I get on Josh's team and you can have Willie. Fair enough?"

"So it's the Feebs versus us champions," Ryan observed.

"Feebs versus Fatheads," Josh corrected. "Let's play. Our out."

Ryan bounced the ball over to Josh who stepped outside the green line. Trevor moved onto the court, with an expression of utter boredom on his face. Willie moved into defense, huffing and puffing at the exertion of moving at all. I tried to position myself to receive a pass, but was hemmed in by Ryan, who had certainly learned a thing or two about pushing with his hips.

So had I. A quick shove and I was off, around him, zooming across from Josh who passed the ball right where I wanted it. I grabbed the ball, pivoted, watched Ryan barreling down on me, then bounce-passed right past him to Skye who went for an easy lay-up. Two points for Feebs. Skye's gold tooth was shining as he smiled.

"Yeah, well, we weren't ready," Ryan muttered.

"Sure," Josh said. "Your out. Two-nothing, us."

"Hey, what about all those points we had?" Ryan complained.

Josh shook his head, looking like a small mountain in the middle of the basketball court. "That was last game. This game it's two-nothing, Feebs. Your out, Fathead."

Ryan was seething. He stepped outside the green line, passed to Arnie who dribbled past Skye but got stopped by me. Arnie passed back to Ryan who dribbled past Josh, and used Willie as a screen to get around Skye. Ryan was ready to shoot when I jumped in front of him, pushing the ball out of his hands.

I heard a vague "What?" of surprise, but there was no time to get into a long discourse on the capacity of short people to jump. Josh picked up the ball, called out, "Take it back" to Jason who dribbled to half-court, then passed to Skye at the left. We did a three lane fast break, Skye at the left, Josh in the middle, me at the right. Skye to Josh: boom; Josh to me: boom. Skye breaks free; pass to him. Up and in.

"All right, man," Skye said, giving me a high-five.

"Reverse it next time, before they get the pattern," I said, repeating Pro's words almost to the letter.

Eduardo took the ball out for the Fatheads and passed it to Ryan. Willie was in the key, looking helpless but ready to shoot the ball if it ever made it to him. Bruce was under the basket, guarded by both Trevor and me. Arnie made a break down the left, received the pass from Ryan and was ready to move in, using Willie as a screen. So I stepped into the hole as Arnie kept on coming, oblivious to my presence, dribble-step, dribble-step, dribble-crash.

He came into me, full force, and sent me flying. His shoulder connected first, thudding up into my chin, pushing my lower jaw up into my tongue and upper teeth. Crunch. Flying backwards and up, then down on the floor, my mouth filled with the metallic taste of blood.

"Charging," Josh called out. "Our ball." Actually, we already had the ball since Arnie had lost it after plowing into me, but my not-so-graceful flight and fall had already stopped the game and demanded some kind of call. "You okay, Moonkid?" Josh asked, looking down on me.

I stared up at the curious and/or concerned faces of Josh, Skye, Steve and Trevor. Then I smiled. "Just a little blood," I told them. "Doesn't Newman always say that basketball is a contact sport? Let's play."

It was more than a little blood. I had taken a fair chunk out of my tongue and managed in the next few minutes to leave blobs of blood on the polished wooden floor, on my own T-shirt and on any members of the other team who came within drooling distance. This acted as a deterrent against further aggression, and we were able to play a fairly civilized game for some period of time. Eventually the Fatheads figured out our one play, the fast break, and managed to stop it with a full-court press. Eventually, too, they figured out that fat Willie could shoot better than any other man on their team, so all they had to do was set him up, to get a couple points.

The result was something like a tie, at least Josh said it was 18-18, and the Fatheads didn't pretend it was very much different.

By that time, I was no longer losing blood but was feeling a bit lightheaded. While my basketball skills had improved over the last six weeks or so, my fitness level hadn't changed all that much. I'd moved from vegetable to milquetoast, maybe, but certainly not up to average, or anywhere near Ryan's aerobic superstar. As I flagged, he ran faster. The only real prayer for us Feebs was the clock. Only five minutes left to go until we hit the showers.

"Steve, you take it out," Josh wheezed. Even he was getting tired, this far past the peak conditioning of football season.

Steve stepped out-of-bounds, harassed by Eduardo, and finally managed a bounce pass to Skye. Skye went to the center, looking for someone to weave in for the ball, but we were all so tired that nothing was working. Eventually Skye took a shot from too far back and missed. I went up for the rebound and managed to grab the ball. At the same time, I felt a clunk on my head. I knelt

250

down, shielding the ball with my body, while more blood rushed into my mouth. Ryan climbed all over me, fouling me half a dozen times in half as many seconds, while various voices shouted, "Here! Behind you! Here!" I pivoted, faked a pass to Skye to throw Ryan off guard, then fell back and aimed at the sweet spot. This was it, the shot that counted. Take a breath, aim, shoot.

Bounce and in.

"Way to go, Moonkid!" Skye shouted.

"Twenty-eighteen. Us," Josh pronounced.

"He fouled me!" Ryan shouted, getting the facts entirely reversed.

"Shut up and play," Josh told him, tossing the ball to Arnie, who was on the green line.

Arnie tossed to Eduardo while Ryan continued muttering. The two teammates got the ball into play, then tried a pass to Willie that didn't work. Skye and Ryan ended up fighting over the loose ball, then I charged in, drooling blood on both of them. Ryan swore, grabbed the ball away, took three steps and shot.

"Traveling," Skye called, even before the ball went in.

"Steps," I echoed.

"No way. It was one and a half," Ryan said defensively. "Two points. Tie."

There followed some discussion between Skye and Ryan about their respective births, parentage and sexual preferences, an argument that I feared might cause Skye to escalate from mere armed robbery all the way to second-degree murder. Josh cut it off. "We haven't got time for this. Call it a tie. Next basket takes it."

Skye and Ryan stopped staring at each other, pulled back, looked at the clock and decided to continue the game. It was our out.

Josh stepped back behind the green line, tossed the ball to Steve who dribbled twice and then passed to Skye. The game was moving fast now: the last point, the ball in our possession. Skye bounce-passed to Josh, who missed it, but I recovered the ball. Ryan and Eduardo were on top of me, grabbing at the ball like eagles clawing at someone attacking their nest. I couldn't get the ball out and somebody was counting time. The only clear shot was to Trevor, who looked panicked at the thought that I might throw to him. Alas, I had no choice. I literally rolled the ball to Trevor. He picked it up, realized he was in the clear and took a shot.

Not even close.

Bruce took it out for their side, managed to get it to Eduardo who passed to Willie, but Josh was all over him, so he passed to Ryan. I could see the move coming: Ryan dribbling past Eduardo, using Trevor as a screen, then going up for the jump shot. If I put myself right there it would stop him.

Make that, it *ought* to stop him. Ryan came

charging forward, past Trevor, into the hole and right into me. Boom, I was down and bleeding again. The ball had rolled out of bounds.

"Now that's a foul," Josh called. "I say Ian gets a foul shot!"

"Foul shot! No way!"

"You charged him, man. You *assaulted* him, you —" Skye went on.

There was some considerable argument going on above my head. At that moment, I didn't want a foul shot nearly as much as I wanted a transfusion, but foul shot was the call. Apparently Skye had convinced Ryan that the game could be ended either with my foul shot or with Skye dicing and slicing Ryan's face in the school parking lot. The foul shot option seemed more attractive.

So I got to my knees, and then to my feet, and then the ball was handed to me. Somewhere at the end of the key loomed the basket, though focusing on it seemed a bit difficult. In the distance, I could hear the supply teacher blowing his whistle and ordering people into the showers. None of us seemed to be paying much attention.

"Two shots," Josh called out. "If either goes in, we win."

"When he misses 'em," Ryan shouted, "we win."

Even with my dismal math skills, this seemed incorrect. The score was tied going into this foul shooting mode. Even if I missed both, the score should at least stay tied. But no one was disagree-ing with Ryan and I was having trouble enough getting two floating images of the basketball hoop to coalesce into one, without worrying about other details.

Josh came up to me. "Just stay calm and aim at the backboard. And stop shaking so much."

I did the best I could on all this, but was proba-bly least successful with the shaking. Calm. Aim over the ball. Take it easy. Up and . . . off the rim.

There was a general moan from our side, a few derisive remarks from the other. Skye threw the ball back to me, giving me a thumbs-up sign I probably didn't deserve. My mind wasn't focused on the game or the ball or Skye, it was on the bleeding in my mouth. If the Red Cross had con-nected a bottle to my tongue, I'd already be on the Top Lifetime Blood Donor list. As it was, I could feel blood dripping down the side of my chin.

"Look at Dracula," Ryan laughed. His team-mates joined in, obviously to distract me.

I looked at them, lined up beside the key, and decided there was only one thing to do. I lifted the ball to my face and wiped my blood with it.

"Oh, gross," Trevor called out, but the rest of my team applauded.

My vision cleared, and the two baskets came together. I lifted the bloody ball, aimed a little higher, set the ball free and waited for the basket.

Swish. Didn't even touch the rim. Game for us.

Now it was my team that was all over me, Skye pounding my back and Josh shaking my hand, Steve and Jason almost carrying me to the showers. Even Trevor seemed happy with the victory. The Feebs left the gym as champions, the Fatheads grunting and groaning behind us about alleged rule violations and the utter grossness of smearing bloody drool on a basketball. Finally, I told Ryan that he was nothing but a bubonic dog scrotum, an insult that shut him up and brought a cheer from my team. *"Feebs forever. We are the Feebs. We are the champions."*

It was only after the shower, after I had washed away most of the taste of blood, that Josh and Arnie came over beside me. I was getting into my number 42 jacket, feeling quite a bit more radiant than at any other time in my brief life on this planet. And then things got brighter still.

"You played a good game, Moonkid," Arnie said. This seemed a special tribute coming, as it did, from a member of the other team.

"Yeah, I've been practicing."

"You took a lot of punishment," Josh said. "I know guys on the football team who couldn't stand up to all that."

I smiled. I had barely stood up to it myself, but there was no sense reinforcing my 'feeb' stereotype.

"Anyway, there's a party at Gen's Saturday night. Thought you might want to come."

"Gen's?" I asked, stupidly. Blood loss does that to you.

"Genevieve Boucher," Josh explained. "You know her. And Jessica. Your locker's right next to 'em."

"Oh, right," I said, all this slowly sinking in. "A party . . . "

"Gen's parents are away some place, so it should be good," Arnie went on. "I'll talk to her so she knows you're coming. Any time after nine, ten. You know."

"Yeah, sure," I said.

"You played great," Josh said, slapping me on the shoulder again. By now this was beginning to hurt. "Nice to see that you're really one of us."

And then the two of them went off as I stood there, stunned. A party. I had never been invited to a party before. A few times I had attempted to crash parties. Once the police were called to remove me from the front porch of a house in Mt. Forest where there was a party going on but nobody wanted me even near it. I had even created one party of my own, in honor of St. Lucy's day, to which two dozen kids were invited but only Libby and R.T. actually showed up.

But here I was invited to a party with Genevieve Boucher, one of the Lord's gifts to the world of men, and her equally bodacious friend Jessica Smith-Weir. Me! This miserable, marooned yet suddenly marvelous Moonkid!

Except it was Saturday night. There was something about Saturday night . . .

Prometheus! I'd promised to go to some stupid wrestling match with Pro!

Chapter 32

When I walked back to my house, I could see the light on in Libby's room. I was surprised to find her home, since mostly she stayed at the university until thirty seconds before supper. My father, as usual, was at the store until closing it up at seven, so Libby must have had some reason to be home early.

I went in the front door, slamming it and pounding my feet, just in case she had brought a new boyfriend home for a few minutes of illicit delight. But the sounds upstairs were more of the scraping-chairs variety. After a decent interval, I walked up the stairs and saw that her door was open.

"Lib?" I said, coming down the hall. "You home?"

"No, I'm an idiot burglar who doesn't know

enough to keep the noise down," she replied. "Ian, you really are slow."

I got to the door and looked inside. Libby was standing beside a stack of eight liquor-store boxes, about to drop a pile of paperback books into one of them.

"What are you doing?" I said, stupidly.

"Packing. I'm out of here in a month, and I got these boxes, so I'm starting." Libby had a flabbergasted look on her face, a combination of a frown and a peculiar shape to her mouth that made her look like Melanie Griffith sucking a lollipop. "This is the pits, Ian. I've been collecting garbage for nineteen years and now I have to figure out what stays and what goes. It's like my whole dusty life is passing before my eyes, or through my hands, or whatever."

"I guess."

"So what's the matter with you?" she said, picking up Muffin, her stuffed bear, to put him in a box, and then deciding otherwise. "You look like you got run over by a truck." She paused to study my face more closely. "Your lip's all swollen up, Ian. You get in a fight, or what?"

"No, I played basketball. We won," I said.

"If winning the game did that to you, I'm glad you didn't lose." Libby went over to put Muffin back on her bed, then grabbed a handful of books from her shelves. "Maybe that Prometheus kid will overcome your genetics and turn you into an athlete."

"Not likely. But I played really well, and when the game was over I got invited to a party."

Libby dropped the books into a box. *Kathunk*. "You? Invited to a party? Was this some kind of joke or something?"

"No joke," I said, sitting down on the edge of her bed. I suddenly felt tired, weary to my bones. "I guess I'm not as weird as I used to be."

"Trust me, Ian, you're every bit as weird," Libby replied. "You just hide it better. Like some kind of psychological acne cream, it covers up the zits of your personality."

"Thanks, Lib, I needed that."

"Okay, sorry," she said, flopping down into the chair by her desk. "Maybe you're learning to be a little less obnoxious. I don't know. I haven't seen you much lately. So congratulations, have a good time. You need me to teach you how to dance or something?"

"No, I need you to give me some advice," I said. Somehow the last word stuck in my throat and came out sounding strange.

"This is truly amazing," Libby replied. "The last time you asked for my advice was . . . Wasn't it back in grade six when Freddy Waterman called you a goof and you wanted to know whether to punch him in the nose or blow up his house with dynamite?"

"And you pointed out that I didn't have any dynamite," I said. "But this time I'm serious. Like

I said, I've got this party on Saturday but last week I told Prometheus I'd go with him to a wrestling match way out in the boonies."

"And you really want to go to the party?" Libby asked.

"Yeah."

"And there's only one night for the wrestling match?"

"Yeah."

"And Prometheus is counting on you to go to this wrestling match?"

"Yeah. I think it's important to him. I don't know why. And he's my friend, kind of. Well, he is."

"Then you've answered your own question, Ian. Friends count, parties don't. Have fun at the wrestling match." She leaned back in the chair, smiling at me as she had so often in the past, with that mixture of mockery and affection, the one obvious, the other not so easy to detect.

I sat on the bed, looking at her, looking at the boxes and the half-empty bookcase, and suddenly felt this enormous wave of emotion, like some kind of tidal wave that had started months ago in the deeper waters of my soul.

"Ian, you're crying," Libby said, surprised. She got up and sat next to me on the bed. "Did you really get hurt today? Did I say something . . . ?"

I shook my head — no, no. I couldn't speak. There was a lump in my chest that constricted my throat and made the beating of my heart painful.

There was some terrible glob of feeling down there, lodged inside me, that just had to get out.

Libby ran her hand over my head, the way she used to when we were little and somebody would beat me up, and I'd race home in rage and anger and fear and pain. Libby would always be there to run her hand over my head, smoothing the hair, soothing the hurt.

I buried my face in both hands, the tears coming faster, my chest heaving. I felt like such a suck. None of this made any sense. I was a champion, I was a fine tutor, I was a good friend, I had heart. But maybe my heart was a problem in all this. Maybe my heart had something to say.

"It's all right, Ian. It's all right . . . " It was Libby's quieting voice, the one I had heard so often because I never really had a mother, or a mother I could count on. I just had Libby and maybe that was enough. Except for one more terrible thing.

"Libby," I said, the consonants all blubbery, "Libby, I'm going to miss you."

Chapter 33

My journal #8. December 3

It's a funny thing how we care about people even when it ~~don t~~ doesn't make any sense. Like my old man. Last time I saw him I told him I never ever wanted to see him again. Of course, that time was pretty bad, him hitting Tina and Mama and the police coming. He was a drunk, then. He was this old, fat, washed-out wrestler that didn't have ~~noth ing~~ anything going for him. I guess maybe I even feel sorry for him now, a little. But back when I was 8, I was just scared. My old man's a big guy and when he gets going you ~~gotta~~ have to watch out for yourself. But that was five years ago, and now I'm big enough to look after myself. Okay, maybe I'm not big enough to take on Mount

Olympus yet, but I'm getting there. And besides, he's getting old.

So how can he still wrestle? That's what I want to know. Last time I ~~seen~~ saw him he was this old fat drunk guy, without a hope. Then there was a couple phone calls, you know the kind, like he's all ~~ref~~ reformed all of a sudden. Sure. I wouldn't even talk to him after what he ~~done~~ did to us all.

And now he's back in the ring. Can you beat that? A big comeback match, that's what they said on the poster. Even saw a ~~comer~~ ~~comm~~ ad on TV on Saturday. Somebody must have dried out my old man, is what I think. But I kind of wonder how good he's ~~gonna~~ going to do? That Crusher guy looked pretty mean on TV. My ~~dad~~ old man only looks mean when he gets drunk.

Moonkid's going to come with me. I guess he's kind of my friend now. That's what I mean about how funny it is the way we care about people. I guess Moonkid cares about me, but how come? There's no reason. He ~~aint~~ isn't family or a kid or even black. He's just this weird dude with a weird family ~~whose~~ who's kind of a spaz, but he's still my friend. Sometimes I think I like him more than Tina or Amos. How's that for strange? Maybe Moonkid is rubbing off on me and I'm getting weird too.

Guess that's enough about all this. The wrestling match has got me thinking about a lot of stupid stuff, so I'm kind of running off at the *mouth. No, I'm running off at the pen. How about that for a bad joke? Just like Moonkid. The guy is ~~contag~~ contagious (had to look that one up for sure).*

Hope my old man wins. But what ~~diffr differance~~ difference does it make. Why should ~~I give a do~~ I care any?

Chapter 34

We bounced along on a bus way out in Woodside, one of those urban-sprawl communities, where the main streets are dotted with all-night gas bars, strip malls, video stores and ceiling fan factory outlets. Not to mention competing Becker's and Mac's Milk stores, the odd 1950's industrial building and many wide stretches of land awaiting similar beautification.

"How come this match is out here in the boonies? I thought wrestling was down at the Gardens," I said, more than a little annoyed to be bouncing on a bus when I could have been talking to Josh and the guys. Or gazing into Gen Boucher's eyes, or staring right at Jessica Smith-Weir's navel.

Prometheus broke into my thoughts. "That's big-time wrestling. WWF."

Pro looked positively enormous in his winter parka. It's amazing how fast most human kids grow when they're thirteen. Unfortunately, aliens seem to miss that particular growth spurt and spend the rest of their days the same size as a fire hydrant.

"So what's this?"

"Small-time wrestling. Some local guy put it together. See," he said, pulling out a handbill. "Only two real names on the bill — Jack Flash and that guy Okimoto. The rest of these guys, they're . . . nobody."

"So you follow wrestling, I guess."

"Keep an eye on it," Prometheus said. "Might end up a wrestler myself if I don't make it to university."

Given his likely size in a year or two, that wasn't an unreasonable fall-back idea. Could be a tough part-time job, though. "What if you get to university?"

"Been thinkin' about bein' a teacher," he said, looking absently out the window. "Kind of like Ms. Noble, you know, work with the toughest kids, teach 'em all the great stuff there is. But then I think maybe I wanna be a cop like on TV. But yesterday, a couple cops came and took Zed off to this detention center place, and that don't seem like such a smart thing, you know? Gonna take this kid who's just kind of mouthy and turn him into a real con. That ain't the way to go. And I don't even like Zed, or the guys in that gang, but

it still seems dumb. So I can't make up my mind."
He seemed to be thinking about all that before he
came back to me. "What you wanna be, Moonkid?"

"How about a career in the NBA?"

Prometheus smiled. "I mean, for real."

"Maybe a writer," I said, smiling a bit at the
thought of sitting in some garret, hunched over a
manuscript with my quill pen in hand. Okay, so
maybe I'd be hunched over a computer, but the
garret was definitely important.

"You'd be good," Pro said. "You spell real good."

Better add a dictionary to my garret, I thought
to myself.

The bus lurched to a stop at the Civic Centre, a
strange modern building that was obviously
designed by an architect who had spent many
years working with Lego. According to the sign,
Woodside's Civic Centre housed the City Hall, the
local courts, a library, what was to be a YMCA,
two day care centers, local branches of AA and Al-
Anon, an art gallery and some kind of community
gymnasium which had apparently been given over
to wrestling for the night.

Prometheus had already bought the tickets
someplace, insisting that this was his treat. He held
them in his hand as we made our way forward in
the line to get in.

We entered what was either an upscale gym or
downscale auditorium, the kind of enormous room
that could be used for everything from beauty

pageants to chamber music recitals. The participants, unfortunately, would have to put up with a general aroma of decaying polystyrene tinged with body odor, and the kind of acoustics one would expect in a submarine.

For this particular evening, the place had been set up with a makeshift wrestling ring in the middle of the floor. It was surrounded by chairs arranged by color to match the price of the ticket. Pulled-out bleacher seats went up each wall. There was some raucous music that was neither pop nor rap nor elevator blaring from speakers mounted over the ring. Off to one side was a refreshment stand, adding its own smell of popcorn and spilled drinks to the general ambiance.

Prometheus and I made our way to our seats close to the front, near a bunch of hyperactive kids who ought to have been put on Ritalin, and some paunchy fathers of the "wanna-come-to-the-beer-store-in-my-new-Magicwagon" variety. Generally speaking, there was an absence of glamour that made the whole enterprise rather seedy. Just what I'd always suspected about wrestling, prizefighting, feeding Christians to the lions and the other proletarian spectator sports. And I had given up Gen Boucher's party . . . for this.

Prometheus had been to such events before, he told me, back in some distant past that never became very clear. Apparently he had gone regularly to Maple Leaf Gardens to watch wrestling when he was a kid, but given it up a few years ago. Our actual reason for coming all the way to Woodside was never spelled out. Prometheus muttered, "Something for my journal" and, "Don't worry, I'm paying," when I pressed him on it. Nonetheless, I had a hunch. I may be socially challenged, but I'm not a social idiot any more.

"First match is this guy Cee-zar Nicholas versus The Turk," Prometheus said, reading the program.

"It's *zar*," I said. "Czar is like the king of Russia."

"Sure spell it funny."

"Sometimes they spell it t-s-a-r. Maybe it makes sense if you speak Russian. You know the old joke, if the king of Russia is the czar and the queen is a czarina, what do they call the kids?"

"I dunno. What?"

"Czardines."

"That's bad," Prometheus agreed, but he smiled anyhow.

Heavy music began pumping through the speakers overhead and it looked like our evening's entertainment was about to begin. Then came the voice, one of those booming, hyped-up announcer voices that are supposed to bring on the excitement. It didn't seem to be working. All I saw was a bunch of confused kids bombarded by the noise, some fathers and mothers looking harassed, a few bored teenagers who were probably only there because the tickets were cheap, and one or two heavily-muscled individuals of both sexes who must have shown up for career planning.

In the ring appeared two gentlemen who were obviously not wrestlers. One was in black tie, one in a short-sleeved shirt. I took the first to be the announcer and the second to be the referee. Right on both counts. The announcer tried hard to pump up the audience, but only succeeded in getting a few minor cheers from the younger set. The rest of the group, I suppose, were waiting for blood. They wouldn't be disappointed.

"AND HERE HE COMES, LADIES AND GENTLEMEN, BOYS AND GIRLS, DIRECT FROM MOSCOW AND LENINGRAD, THE FINEST WRESTLER FROM WHAT USED TO BE THE COMMUNIST WORLD — (dynamic pause) — CZAAAR NICHOLAS."

There was a crescendo of noise passing for music, a few cheers and/or boos from some of the fans. Then from one corner of the gym, a large man in red tights emerged. A hammer-and-sickle was embroidered on one his thighs, for reasons that made no historical sense. He was sporting a pair of arms that looked oiled with Mazola.

"AND HIS OPPONENT, THE WILY, UNPREDICTABLE AND TOTALLY DANGEROUS MAN FROM THE MIDDLE EAST — THE TUUURK!"

"This going to be any good?" I asked.

"Probably not," Pro answered over the noise.

"First match is usually the worst. Young guys who don't know how to put on a show or old guys over the hill. Kind of a warm-up."

"Want some popcorn?" I asked.

"Not me, man. Sticks between my teeth."

We settled in to watch the match. Pro had gotten good seats, down on the floor, not too far from the metal railings that surrounded the ring. The metal railings were there to do what the red, white, and blue ring ropes could not — hold in the wrestlers.

The match began with an enormous amount of sweating, grimacing, screaming and thumping. But it didn't really get interesting until The Turk sent Czar Nicholas flying over the ropes and onto the floor. The enormous man landed with a thud like an elephant falling from the cargo bay of a jet aircraft.

"Is he hurt?" I asked.

"Probably not," Pro told me. "They plan those pretty good."

Apparently so. Czar Nicholas got up on his feet, shook his head, and then went charging back into the ring. He bounced against the ropes on three sides and then went hurling right into The Turk, who fell backwards onto the floor.

By now the audience had got what it paid for: pain, sweat, excitement, theater! The little kids were screaming and shouting in their charming way, "Kill him! Smash him! Stomp his face!" Even the dads, fresh from their Magicwagons, were shouting encouragement to either the Czar or The Turk, or perhaps both at once. None of the screaming made much difference, because The Turk stayed on the mat for the requisite three seconds and Czar Nicholas was declared the victor. Perhaps it was some consolation for his namesake's cruel fate in history.

"What'cha think?" Prometheus asked as the sweaty wrestlers made their way down the aisles.

"These guys could be dangerous," I said.

"Wrestlers are all big, man, every one of 'em."

"I don't mean the wrestlers," I corrected. "I mean the crowd."

It is the human propensity for violence that has always bothered me most about the species. All right, my species, if I have to admit it. I can understand necessary violence — taking out a splinter, or resetting a broken bone, perhaps even spanking a child — but I cannot understand how they — all right, we — glory in gratuitous violence. Football, Serbia, hockey, Northern Ireland, soccer, most movies: I could develop a long, long list. What is there about us that brings smiles to our faces when someone else is suffering? What is it that makes the blood rush when one oversized man is pounding, pummeling or twisting the daylights out of another poor oversized man? Why were all the little kids in the audience shouting, their cheeks glowing red, their hearts pumping faster, as Czar Nicholas turned into a human cannonball? What is wrong with us?

Pro broke into my thoughts. "It gets better, each match. Just wait."

We didn't have to wait long. After a musical interlude that probably made aspirin a best-seller at the concession stand, the tag-team match began. It featured the Canucks, dressed in red-and-white maple leaf costumes, against the Moto Brothers, two large Orientals who looked like Sumo wrestlers.

Watching the match taught me one thing. Canadian patriotism, so much belittled in the press, is alive and well at wrestling arenas. The Canucks pounded, slapped, carried, whipped, and otherwise throttled the Moto Brothers, who used their enormous size advantage to simply ignore the assault. They stood like giant statues of Buddha attacked by mosquitoes.

The crowd responded nationalistically, by getting more and more angry. You could see it in their faces as the collective F&I index rose: bared teeth, straining eyes, tense foreheads, dilated nostrils. Even Prometheus, who prides himself on his cool, was shouting for justice, raising a fist into the air calling for more violence. Finally the cries of the crowd were rewarded. Both Canucks climbed into the ring at one time to take on a lone Moto, while their manager, a fellow dressed in a pseudo-Ronald McDonald outfit, managed to delay the other Moto. The result was a sweaty, grunting atrocity that put the first Mr. Moto on the mat and gave the victory to Canada.

"How'd you like that?" Pro asked.

"It wasn't fair. The Canucks were two against one. Is that what it takes to beat the Japanese? Two hockey players to one Sumo wrestler?"

"It's just a show, man. Don't take it so serious," Pro smiled.

"Seriously," I corrected.

"Don't take it like that, neither."

"So what's next? *Mount Olympus does a comeback against The Crusher*," I read from the program. "Sounds like Greek gods trying to take on modern technology."

"That Mount Olympus guy, he used to be good," Prometheus said, his smile disappearing.

"You know him?"

"Seen him," Pro corrected.

"What about The Crusher?"

"He's new. Look."

At one corner of the ring, accompanied by a musical drum roll that sounded a lot like a bull-dozer crushing violins, appeared the man in question.

"AND NOW, IN A MATCH TO KEEP HIS TITLE AND HIS HONOR, THE REIGNING CHAMPION IN CANADA'S HEAVYWEIGHT DIVISION, LADIES AND GENTLEMEN, BOYS AND GIRLS, THE CRUUUUSHER!"

The Crusher lived up to his heavyweight billing, probably pushing four hundred pounds. His outfit drew its colors from an International Harvester earth mover: yellow for the singlet, a black leather toque for his head. Like all the wrestlers, he was well-oiled with what must have been, given his name, 10W30. Apparently he had fans in the audience, because any number of little kids were growling in appreciation, like earth movers on a highway job.

"AND HIS OPPONENT, MAKING A STRONG COMEBACK BID THIS YEAR, THE FORMER HEAVYWEIGHT CHAMPION AND STAR . . . NONE OTHER THAN THE FAMOUS, THE HEROIC . . . MOUNT OLYMMMPUS!"

The speaker overhead began blaring out music from *The Ride of the Valkyries*. This obvious confusion of Greek and German gods was augmented by Mount Olympus himself, whose costume included a Viking hat and white fur jacket. Both looked a bit absurd on this enormous black man, and neither suggested the ancient glories of Greece. I suspected that Mount Olympus was a low-rent act, set up to take the fall from the more popular and better-outfitted Crusher. From the attitude of the kids around us, Mount Olympus must have lost most of his fans along with his title some years back. The loudest cheering, in fact, came from Prometheus.

I turned to him. "You must like this guy."

Prometheus shrugged. "Us Greek gods got something in common."

The two giants lumbered into the ring, their managers trailing behind them like clowns or court jesters. After the usual preliminaries, the match began. The somewhat king-sized Crusher stood in the middle, as Mount Olympus went bouncing against the rings and then into, above and under his opponent. It was almost as if the whole match were choreographed in advance, an overweight *pas de deux* accompanied not by Tchaikovsky but by slaps, screams and groans.

"That's pretty fake," I said.

"Yeah," Pro agreed. "They practice it up."

I was going to say something like, how do you know, but the action on stage was heating up. The Crusher, apparently riled by Mount Olympus' bouncing charges, was counterattacking with some heavy-duty thumping to Olympus' neck. Each thump was accompanied by a cheer from the sadistic audience. More interesting to me, though, was the way Prometheus twisted his neck each time Mount Olympus got hit.

"Pro —" I began.

"Shut up. I wanna watch."

Eventually Mount Olympus broke free and resumed his bouncing routine against the ropes, managing to flatten The Crusher with a manoeuvre they call the clothesline. The Crusher got back to his feet, perhaps encouraged by screaming good wishes from his fans — "Get up, you slob! Kill him! Smash his head!" — and proceeded with an attack against Mount Olympus that actually involved some wrestling. I observed an arm lock and a hammer lock, even before The Crusher shifted to a martial arts kick.

The kick sent Mount Olympus to the mat, grimacing in what might have been real pain. Prometheus, beside me, had a similar expression on his face: clenched teeth, sweaty cheeks, sheer concentration about the eyes.

Mount Olympus was down for two seconds, amid boos and cries of derision from the audience, but then leapt back to his feet. He looked up at the lights and held his arms up high, as if receiving a boost in power from Zeus or whatever god was currently supervising the Woodside Civic Centre. This quasi-religious ritual complete, he bounced against one rope, hurled into The Crusher, dazed him, caught the man with two hands and flipped him right out of the ring.

"Way to go!" Prometheus shouted.

Reaction from the rest of the audience was mixed: hissing and clapping, shrieking and cheering. Mount Olympus pranced around the ring, his arms lifted triumphantly, while The Crusher climbed back in. He looked exhausted, like an International Harvester tractor after a long day on the job.

Mount Olympus bounced against two sets of

ropes, smashed into The Crusher, then thumped him on the back of the head to take him down. While The Crusher was still on the mat and the audience was screaming for their hero to get up, Mount Olympus climbed on top of one of the corner posts, raised one hand to the gods, and jumped right on The Crusher's head. Or so it seemed. Actually, The Crusher seemed to take little real damage from this, but he made no effort to get up from the mat.

The match was soon over. Amid boos and screams from the crowd, the ref counted The Crusher down and then lifted Mount Olympus' arm in triumph.

I turned to see what Prometheus thought of all this, but I was too late. He was already on his feet and making his way down to the metal railings that kept the audience away from the wrestlers. Even before I could get halfway there, Prometheus had pushed his way right up to the railing.

I made my way through the crowd as best I could, finally pushing my way in beside Prometheus as Mount Olympus came down the aisle with his manager. This was adulation time, as the various kids who had booed or hissed at Olympus before now crowded against the rail to get a wave or a nod from the winner. The noise level was incredible. Over the music and the cheering and the stomping of feet, Prometheus had to yell to be heard.

"Pa! Pa, it's me!"

Mount Olympus caught the second shout. He stopped and focused on the crowd. "Pro?"

Time should have stopped. In a film, you can take a moment like that and run it over and over, showing both faces, taking the smile in slow motion, shutting down the sound of the crowd. In life, we only have a second or two, a look, a smile, a nod, a few words.

"Pa, you did good."

And then time moves on. The manager takes his wrestler by the arm and moves him along out of the arena. An announcer reminds fans they can buy popcorn and drinks; the music powers up again for the next match; the fans go back to their seats. But for one, or two, or three of us, everything is a little different.

Chapter 35

My journal # 9. December 8

My ~~old man~~ dad won! He's coming back, really!
This wrestling stuff is all so ~~fony~~ phoney, but I
still felt great when he beat The Crusher. I felt like
shouting out to everybody, hey, it's my old man, he
won! Of course I'm too cool for that, but I was still
plenty proud of him. He wrestled ~~good~~ well and
put on a good show. Now if he can just keep off the
booze and the dope, maybe he'll do okay.

Moonkid said he had a hunch Mount Olympus
was my dad or somebody special. He said there's
no other reason to go all the way to Woodside
unless it was something like that. Of course,
Moonkid likes to think he knows everything, but it
was still good having him there. After I told my

dad he did so ~~good~~ well, Moonkid said I was crying. So I said, why not? You got to cry when big stuff happens in your life, or else you can't really feel it deep down. Sometimes I think Moonkid acts like a stupid little kid who only cries when his head gets punched in. If I got to cry, I want it to be because I'm real happy. Or maybe real sad, but you get the idea. It's for important stuff.

My dad called up today and asked if he could see me and Amos. I said okay and my mom said okay and Amos said okay but he can't even remember the guy. Next weekend we're going to Ajax where my dad lives now. He says he's really got his life ~~straten~~ straightened around, and I believe him. He couldn't beat The Crusher if he was still a ~~reck~~ wreck like he used to be. Bet he's even got a girlfriend. We'll find out next week.

Tina's moving in with this guy she met. She says they're engaged and she's even got a ring, but I don't think it's a real ~~dimond~~ diamond. Mama's all happy about that and I guess I am too. At least I won't have to worry about Z-boy and his gang giving her a hard time because of what she used to be.

Amos just watches TV all the time, and it bugs me. I got to get some books from the library and read something to him so he won't grow up stupid. He ought to grow up so old Mount Olympus can be proud of him, not some kind of reject like Z-boy. I said to Amos, if you end up hanging around the *park like those guys, I'm going to kill you first. Maybe that'll get it into his head. But I got to start reading to him soon because his teacher says he's in the bottom quartile. What's a quartile? It's not even in my dictionary. Must be bad, that's all I can figure.*

Moonkid says he's getting really good at basketball, but I said, don't let it go to your head, your ears'll get even bigger than they are now. He laughed. Moonkid gave up going to a party to come to the wrestling match, so I guess I owe him one. He wants me to go to the airport when his sister takes off for ~~Calf~~ ~~Cal~~ ~~Califfo~~ her mom's place, so I said okay. Like I say, I owe him one. And he's my friend.

Chapter 36

My father and his girlfriend Margaret drove Libby to the airport in Margaret's car, the world's oldest surviving Volkswagen van. Even with two-thirds of Libby's earthly possessions stored in the basement or out in the garbage, the remaining boxes and suitcases took up the whole van. There certainly wasn't enough room for me and a possible future wrestler like Prometheus, so the Airport Express became our means of transportation.

"How you feel?" Pro asked me. He was carrying one of the three books I'd given him for Christmas, a sci-fi book called *Berserker*.

"Fine. I'm fine," I said, repeating myself. I was wearing a plaid scarf that Prometheus had given me, a scarf long enough that I could wrap it several times around my neck.

"Don't look fine. You look kinda sick, if you ask me."

I turned to him. He had that funny expression on his face: not really smiling, but with his forehead all wrinkled up as if he was curious about something. "So did I ask?"

"Guess not." He shrugged. "Listen, it's okay to feel lousy. You love your sister, and you're gonna miss her, that's all."

Love? I thought to myself. *I love my sister?* What a bizarre thought. Libby and I had lived for the last sixteen years with so much heartache, so much confusion, so much frantic effort to survive on this hostile planet that we never stopped to think how we actually felt about each other. Don't they say that people in a disaster go kind of numb? Or maybe the emotions are there, all right, but covered over with something protective and functional. Love wrapped in plastic wrap, love stuffed in a baggie. Or maybe Pro had just picked the wrong word. I wouldn't, myself, have used the word *love* to talk about the relationship between me and Libby. I would have used the word need. Where was she going to be when I *needed* her? That was the question that kept nagging at me.

"So how was the visit with your father?" I asked, not-so-subtly changing the subject.

"Okay," he said, looking forward now. "Went to his place up in Ajax for dinner and met his old lady, name of Merna. He's pretty cool now that he's dried out, you know. Even the wrestling thing is coming back for him. He's got another match in February."

"He looked pretty good in the ring."

"Spends a lot of time training, keeping in shape," Pro went on. "He said maybe some time, we can go down to the gym and work out together, but I wasn't so hot on it."

"How come?"

"Don't know," he said, pausing to think. "Guess I don't much like beatin' up on people. I seen enough of that, you know?"

"I guess."

"Been thinking more and more 'bout being a teacher. Guess I could be a wrestling coach and a teacher, but the teacher thing's gotta come first. Lotta kids out there need help. Lotta kids need help who don't even *know* they need help."

For a second, I wondered if he was talking about me, but there was no time to think it through. The bus was pulling into that complex of roads that lead from one airport terminal to the other. Shortly we were deposited at the Canadian Airlines departure level entrance.

My sister, my father and Margaret were nowhere in sight. There were five lines for passengers with tickets, two lines for passengers needing to buy tickets, and one line for Business Class passengers. We checked them all out. Then we looked in the cafeteria, in the restaurant, in the bar. No Libby. No Rick. No Margaret.

"When's the plane s'pose to leave?" Pro asked.

"Fourteen hundred hours," I replied in airport-talk.

"When's that?"

"Two o'clock. That's an hour away. She's got to be —" And then the obvious came to me. "Come on."

We moved quickly through the row of shops that ran between the national and international departure gates: duty free, magazines, souvenirs, flowers, last-minute gifts, coffee-to-go. The Bookshop. There they all were, in different parts of the store. My father, dressed in his very best jeans and an almost-cool leather vest that Margaret had given him for Christmas, was in the science fiction section, about a third of the way through a Philip José Farmer novel. Margaret, dressed in one of those oversized, flower-print dresses she favors, was in the psychology section looking at a book called *Breaking the Glass Ceiling: and how to avoid the shards of broken glass* by some woman whose initialed university degrees took up as much space as her name. And my sister, a *Cosmopolitan* and a *Scientific American* cradled in one arm, was looking in the business section at a book called *Personal Profit Potential: how to achieve total maximization of your business and yourself.*

Libby was the one who looked up and saw us.

"They're here," she told Margaret and my father, who proceeded to put down their books as we came into the store. "Glad you could make it," she said to me.

I shook my head. Why was it that everything we said to each other seemed to be tinged with sarcasm?

"Nice to see you again, Libby," Prometheus said, ignoring her comment.

"We were getting worried," Margaret said, then looked at my father and corrected, "Well, Libby and I were getting worried. She has to get on the plane early, like in ten minutes. There's a customs check."

"You get all her stuff checked in?" I asked.

"Two hundred dollars in excess baggage," my father said, shaking his head. "You'd think she was going for . . . " his words trailed off.

"I am," Libby said. "I'm going for good. This isn't just a visit, you know. I'm going to school out there, like for three more years." There was irritation in her voice, as if she had spent considerable amounts of time trying to drive this simple truth into my father's Jurassic skull.

The three of us were awkward and nervous. My father had this sheepish little-boy look, the kind of expression we used to see when Granny would lecture him, or the cops would arrive at the door for a search. Libby had her mouth set firm, her lips compressed, with a look of determination that reminded me of my mother. And I kept my eyes mostly on my feet, which are relatively oversized and misshapen, in wet Converse basketball shoes that were stained by the snow and slush outside.

It took a sensible voice to break the tension. "Well, you people had better hustle up and say some goodbyes. You don't got much time now," Pro said.

The rest of us looked over at Pro to see him smiling benignly, like a Bill-Cosby-style father grinning at his troubled brood.

"Pro's right," Libby said. "Let's get over to the gate."

She abandoned the book, quickly paid for the two magazines, despite my father's efforts to make them a gift, and then led us down the hall towards the departure lounge. When we reached the point where the signs said Passengers Only it was time to stop.

Margaret spoke first. "Do you have everything?"

"Probably not," Libby replied, looking so organized and businesslike. "I'll make up a list of what I need when I unpack, and somebody can send it out."

"You'll come visit," my father said. I wasn't sure if it was a question or a request.

"Sure I will. Mom's got enough points to fly me back this summer, if I want. And Ian, there's a ticket for you to come out this summer for a month. It's up to you."

I nodded. The P.A. system announced a set of departures, including a final pre-boarding call for Libby's flight.

"That's it. I've got to go. Dad . . . "

Libby went over to my father and gave him a hug. He stood there like a Raggedy Andy doll as Libby took him into her arms.

"You're sure you want . . . to do this?" His voice cracked.

"Rick, we've talked about this," Libby said, letting go. "I'll visit this summer. Now you look after Ian, okay?"

My dad nodded, chastised.

"Margaret, you help him, for me. Okay?" Libby said. "And Prometheus, don't let too many kids knock Ian's head in. It's not much of a head, but it's the only one he has."

Pro smiled and Libby turned to me.

"And you, guy," she said, opening her arms. I moved inside them, my head only as high as her neck, Libby holding me for the last time. "You stay out of trouble. I can't protect you from three thousand miles away, you know."

"Yeah, I know," I said, hugging her back.

"And don't take anything I left in the room, and don't read any letters I get, and don't say anything snide or smart or obnoxious if people call, just give them my new number, okay?"

"Okay."

"Promise?"

"Promise."

Then she broke. I could feel her start to shake, feel her breathing choking up, even before the first tear moved down her cheek and moistened my hair. "I'm going to miss you, you jerk," she cried.

"Me too," I said.

We stood there, holding each other, Libby crying, me trying to be strong. I suppose we could have stood like that for a long time, but Margaret started saying it was final call and Libby had to go, and we both knew that was the truth.

"Bye," Libby said, wiping her wet cheeks with one hand. "I'll call. I'll write." She stopped for a second, reached inside her carry-on bag, and pulled out Muffin, her very favorite stuffed bear. "Ian, you take him. He'll look after you. I gotta go."

Then she turned and went off through the automatic departure room doors to the metal detector on the other side. We waited. When the doors opened again, she was gone. The four of us were left standing there, looking vaguely stupid as we stared at three guards, a metal detector and an X-ray scanner.

"Guess your sister wasn't carrying no guns," Pro said, breaking the tension.

"Guess not," I agreed.

"You two going to ride back with us?" Margaret said, by way of invitation.

Prometheus looked at me.

"No, we'll take the bus back," I said. "You and Rick probably want to talk."

Margaret took the hand of my much-deflated father and smiled. "Yeah, we do. See you later."

My dad grunted some kind of goodbye and then went off with Margaret. That left Prometheus and me relatively free for the afternoon.

"What you want to do?" he asked me.

"I want to watch the plane take off," I said. "There's got to be a skydeck or someplace to watch."

The actual skydeck turned out to be a restaurant with a three-dollar minimum charge, each. Fortunately, Prometheus had some money so the two of us were able to sit in the restaurant and drink the most expensive cokes of our collective lives. Down below us, the enormous planes nestled, connected by passenger tubes and umbilical power cords to the terminal. Little jeeps and diesel trucks scurried beneath the jets, carrying strangely-shaped aluminum containers of food and luggage to the waiting planes. The one just to our right was Libby's plane, a Boeing Jumbo 747 whose fuselage looked like an overweight weisswurst.

"I never been on a plane, you know?" Pro said.

"It's no big deal. Kind of like a noisy bus that shows movies," I said.

"Someday I gotta take one and see for myself."

"What are you doing this summer?" I asked.

"Nothing. The usual. What you thinkin' about?"

"Just an idea," I said, not wanting to reveal my brainwave before I'd had a chance to check it out. If Pro could fly out on my mother's frequent flyer points, then he couldn't complain about not paying his own way. And I could just imagine Prometheus at my mother's place in San Francisco. It would be ... beyond adjectives.

"Planes don't mean a whole lot to you, you take 'em so much," Prometheus concluded for me. "You're probably waiting for some rocket to take you to the moon."

"Nothing's on the moon. I want the nearest galaxy," I said.

"Alpha Centauri."

I looked at him.

"I've been reading. Another planetarium show coming up in March, the paper says. Something 'bout astronauts."

I nodded. Libby's plane started pulling away from the passenger tube. In the hundred tiny windows, I couldn't see her face. The plane backed away, pushed by a little diesel truck, then broke free and began moving towards the runway under its own power.

"You're gonna miss her," Prometheus said as the plane pulled out of view. "I kind of miss Tina, and she ain't even nice like Libby is."

"Libby isn't always nice."

"Nobody is," Pro replied. "But you still love 'em."

"Guess I do."

"So you're gonna miss her."

I looked at him. "It won't be so bad," I said. "I got a friend."

So if any aliens were looking down, they would have seen one very large black teenager sitting, smiling, with one relatively small and misshapen white teenager who was holding a tiny stuffed bear. And off in the distance, a Boeing 747 was taking off, an ungainly waddling goose on the ground, but quite beautiful flying in the air, like a rocket heading off into space.